The Smoke Tree

By Stefanie Nici

The Smoke Tree ©Copyright 2019 Stefanie Nici

Cover Art design by Delightful Designs.

This book is dedicated to my husband Anthony,
For your love and support, as well as being the force
behind making all my dreams come true.

Chapter

1

Slowly creeping out of the dressing room Tora winced, seeing her own reflection from under the harsh bright lights of the fitting room mirror. Standing there, less than impressed in a plain blue, short-sleeved, knee-length dress, she'd had enough disappointment for one day.

"I love how that one looks on you Tora," Kate complimented, paying more attention to her cell phone than her friend. Kate was that impatient friend who told you anything to speed things along.

"Stand up straight!" An older woman's voice instructed from the back of the dressing room, sorting through a heap of clothing left behind by the other unhappy women that day. "And don't slouch!"

Taking the woman's advice, Tora took a deep breath, stood up tall, and pulled back her shoulders. Smoothing the wrinkled fabric that collected around her midriff, she hoped to see a difference, but immediately slouched over once more in defeat.

"I'm getting too fat. I look like a giant blueberry muffin in this dress," she complained.

Sulking at her chubby reflection, she wondered how she had let herself go this much. Yes, her hips were a little wider than the summer before, her belly a little paunchier, and her thighs a little thicker. Her skin had taken on that odd whitish, translucent color from being deprived of the sun for a long time. She was still Tora, just more of her.

"And to think, I thought I was fat in my twenties, and didn't want to wear shorts and bathing suits," shaking her head at the irony of it all.

Tora had made herself a personal promise not to gain too much weight. The type of weight that would be hard to take off. There may come a time in a woman's life when self-control goes out the window, and for Tora, this past year was her time.

"That's nonsense Tora. You are the slimmest of the four of us," Kate said of herself and their friends, looking up from her cell phone on and off for a few seconds at a time.

Tora wondered what her friend saw that she didn't, or was this just Kate simply being Kate?

Kate didn't have the healthiest of diets and somehow, she didn't seem to gain weight. Good posture reflected her confidence. It also gave her a longer, taller appearance than her actual height of five foot seven. Her cute little turned-up nose had a way of shaving off a few of her thirty-nine years, as did the freckles stamped across her flawless skin. It was easy for her to be generous with the compliments when she looked and felt younger than her thirty-four-year-old counterpart.

"It's no fun trying on clothes anymore. I gained too much weight and I look - BIG."

"Stop it. You look great!" Kate said, typing one last text and tucking her cell phone away in her handbag.

Tora knew the more weight she gained the longer it would take to lose it, afraid to one day break "The Seal."

The Seal for Tora meant the point of no return. To put on so much weight, it would be too late to turn back. In order to keep the seal intact, she would need to follow a strict diet and exercise. Tora no longer had the discipline nor the energy for that. Staring back at herself today, she knew she was approaching her seal's breaking point.

'She's gonna blow!' her inner voice warned.

"I have to lose weight." Tora said aloud stomping back toward the stall like a bratty child. All she wanted was a simple dress for her birthday dinner. She still had some time to figure it out.

This blue dress was the eighth dress she tried on today and it was not a good fit. Even going up another size wasn't doing the trick. Being too loose in one area, while too tight in another, Tora gave up.

"If I look like this now," Tora said, as she disappeared behind the dressing room door. "What will I look like at fifty? My mother already looks better than me," she griped.

Kate agreed. "Marie does look amazing, especially for her age. I've seen pictures."

"Think about what we are saying. My seventy-five-year-old mother looks better than me!" she huffed from behind the door.

Tora's mom was still active, vibrant, and did not look her age. Having a good figure allowed her to dress fashionable and flattering. It was hard not to cross that line sometimes, being so slim, able to fit into almost everything, it could be tempting to play with fashion. If only Tora took after her mother in that department.

Knowing she was gaining weight at a slow but steady pace, Tora still found it hard to control her eating. Sometimes she would imagine her fit, handsome husband running off one day and she would be too out of shape to catch him. The visualization would continue with Tora, giving up the chase. Sitting at the side of the road, she'd take a big bite out of a donut she pulled out of her jacket pocket. It was a private joke she had with herself, trying to make light of a situation that otherwise made her depressed.

"I have a month," Tora announced, roughly pushing open the door like a bull released into the ring. "I can do this!" she snorted with determination.

"You CAN do this!" Kate cheered in support as they headed out of the fitting room together.

"I CAN do this!"

"You CAN do this!"

"I WILL do this!"

"You WILL do this!"

They chanted, giving each other a high five as they left the store.

"Who came up with the expression fat and happy?" Tora asked as they walked toward Kate's bright yellow Volkswagen Beetle. "Because I'm fat, and I am NOT happy."

"Hungry?" Kate immediately asked.

Stopping in her tracks, Tora looked at her friend in disbelief. "You're joking, right? Did you not hear a thing I've said for the last two hours?"

"Come on, we hardly spend any time together anymore. Before we know it, you will be back to work soon, teaching those little brats you love so much. Let's grab lunch. You can get a salad. Lunch is as fattening as you make it," Kate pleaded her case persuasively.

Being an elementary school teacher, Tora had the luxury of having the entire summer off. Now, almost the end of August, she had to go back to her classroom to prepare for September. This meant less time for herself, her husband, and her friends. Why not enjoy the free time she had left?

"That is true," Tora agreed, finding an excuse to eat. "I can order smart."

"Or, it can be your last hurrah for a while. Your choice," a wild-eyed Kate grinned, shooting Tora a wink before hopping into the driver's seat.

Getting into the car, Tora buckled up and turned to Kate, "You make good points," she laughed as they drove off and out of the parking lot.

Hearing a low rumble. "Your phone is vibrating," Kate said.

"Is it?" Tora asked, digging in her bag. "It is!" she shrieked as the humming got louder the more she dug. "It's Dane," she whispered to Kate after reading the caller ID.

"Hi Dane!" Tora cheerfully greeted her husband on the other line.

"Hey hon, what are you doing?" he asked in a voice filled with as much enthusiasm as Tora.

"Shopping with Kate. Now we're off to lunch."

"Tell Kate I said hello."

Leaning into Kate, "Dane said hello," she whispered.

"Hi, Dane!" Kate yelled out loudly so he could hear her.

Dane and Kate, along with Donna, Ali, and their significant others, had been friends since childhood. They all grew up within blocks from each other. They went to the same schools, attended the same church, allowing them to celebrate many special moments together.

They were so close as children, even their parents became friends. The situation was so ideal; they all partnered up, and once Dane met Tora, their circle was complete.

One couple, Donna and her husband Scott, had since divorced, but the eight of them remained close friends all the same. They all vacationed, spent holidays and various other occasions together like one big happy family, if there was such a thing.

"I'm calling to tell you I have to work late tonight," Dane informed her.

Rolling her eyes, "Again?"

"Yeah, they want me and Sam to look over a few proposals, get a few ducks in a row and be fresh for tomorrow. Big meeting baby. I'm hoping to meet some key people. Please tell me you understand."

Tora did understand. In fact, she had been "understanding" for most nights this past year.

"You have been working so much, Dane."

"I know, I know, but it's for us, babe. Good things will happen," he assured her, as he always did.

Dane had a small construction business on the side which he was trying to grow while he stayed on in his current foreman position at Peters Construction. He was forming relationships with people that would be useful to him when his own business took off was what he would always tell Tora.

"Our future baby!" Referring to his plans for his career with such gusto, and in a way that reminded Tora of a gambler throwing the dice at the craps table. She'd never had a good feeling about it.

She often wondered how Sam's wife felt about all the time spent away from home. Then again, she didn't know if Sam was married. They'd never met, and Tora never asked.

"OK. Call me later." Tora moaned, no choice in eating dinner alone once more.

"I will. Love you."

"Love you too," Tora said, then ended the call. "Dane is working tonight," she whimpered, tossing her cell phone back in her bag.

"Well, now you can bring home whatever you don't finish," Kate said, giving Tora the side eye. "Look on the bright side, you don't have to cook, wash dishes AND you can watch a scary movie," making home alone for the third night this week sound like fun.

Growing up with Dane, Kate knew his likes and dislikes, and she knew that he hated horror movies. He would never admit it, but they gave him nightmares, even as an adult. As a young boy he would pee the bed, and he probably feared if scared enough, he would again. How do you explain peeing the bed at forty years old to your wife? You don't. You avoid watching horror movies.

While it sounded tempting, the half-eaten lunches and dinners were piling up in the fridge. Not to mention all the unhealthy food was contributing to Tora's rapid weight gain.

"This has to be the last of it though. Not only is it fattening, it's expensive," Tora griped. "I really need to make some changes."

"Well, you have to do something for yourself while Dane is taking time away from you," Kate pointed out.

"It's work, Kate. What can I do?"

"Well, I'm just saying. Don't worry about the expense. I'm sure he must be making good money with all the nights he's been out now."

Was that hostility in Kate's voice Tora detected? Not only was it, unlike Kate to talk about Dane in that way, it made Tora uncomfortable. Especially the "don't worry about the expense" comment. Who was the wife here?

Tora found it challenging at times, having friendships that intertwined with her marriage. Without knowing how to address it, Tora ignored it. It didn't only happen with her though. It was also happening within their circle. Little snide remarks, digs, butting into one another's business, but no one ever seemed bothered by it other than Tora. Then again, Tora wasn't what she called, "a day oner," like the others. "The Three Amigas," Kate, Donna, and Ali were all friends from day one. That was the difference.

"You know what? I have to pass on lunch," Tora decided.

Almost blowing the red light, Kate stopped short, and the women jerked forward.

"What? Why? You're not mad at what I said are you?"

Stunned for a moment, Tora shook her head, "No. I'm just not happy with my weight, and after trying on eight dresses, not one looked good. Not even the black one."

Looking at each other, they broke out into a fit of laughter. Women knew if black wasn't cutting it, they really had problems.

"Okay. Okay," Kate agreed. "But I think you look great."

Tora could have two heads, missing teeth, and be dressed in rags, Kate would still say, "I think you look great." That's what friendship was all about, *lying*.

"But it is all about *you,* and how *you* feel," Kate said.

This past summer, all the barbecues, the hamburger buns and hot dog rolls Tora consumed had caught up with her. Donna's homemade potato salad was the group's most requested must have, and all that creamy deli coleslaw and addicting macaroni salad Tora loved had collected miserably all over her body.

She felt as if she was wearing all she ate this past summer, and if you squeezed her, the mayonnaise may come oozing out of her pores. With that nauseating thought, along with her lack of will power, Tora was disgusted with herself.

As the car behind them began to beep, "Green light," Tora said.

Lowering her driver's side window, Kate's long brown hair had taken flight as it was sucked up and out into the wind. It whipped around wildly as she now sped up onto the freeway, taking the shortest route back to their town. A whooshing and whistling sound filled the car and made it impossible to speak or hear.

Tora couldn't help but sense a sudden aloofness coming from Kate, who just moments ago seemed fine. If she were to dwell on it, it would haunt her all day. Figuring Kate had had it with hearing her complaints, Tora sat back to enjoy the ride.

Daydreaming, Tora gazed out of the car window. She thought about doing some cardio exercises when she got home or pushing herself to go to the gym. After all, she was paying for it every month, why not go? As much as she hated the idea, she knew the weight would not take itself off. The gym to her was an acquired taste, much like raw clams. Just the thought of it repulses you, but after that first slippery sucker, you can't stop.

Pulling up in front of Tora's house, "Home sweet home," Kate announced.

Tora's home was sweet. Her friends and neighbors always told her they found it to be the cutest on the block. Yellow and white flowers planted along the front of the house bordered the greenest grass in the whole town due to Dane's persistent upkeep.

It was a hobby, a passion, an obsession Tora felt, but Dane loved the compliments he received on the curb appeal. Some neighbors would even ask advice for their own brown lawns. Dane was happy to share, but for the others, it never worked. Only he seemed to have that special touch.

"I know I tell you this all the time, but I love that tree of yours," Kate said, admiring the large purple hazy tree on the far end of the property near the driveway. "It's a different color every time I see it."

Kate was right. Tora's Smoke Tree would change color throughout the year, making it seem like many trees in one. Growing up, Tora's grandmother always had one in her yard, and Tora took an interest in its mystery.

"I used to think it was magic," Tora giggled, thinking back to her childhood innocence. "The puffy clusters give off a hazy or smoky appearance, but you only get that effect from a distance. It's an illusion."

Shrugging her shoulders, less impressed now knowing the secret to its trickery. "When we bought this house, that was my only must have. That darn tree," she laughed in retrospect as she began exiting the vehicle. "Some women want a laundry room, or a she - shed. Me? I wanted a tree."

"Tora!" Kate called out, summoning her back.

Tora poked her head inside.

"You know you're my best friend, right?"

That was a weird thing to say she thought to herself, causing her to reconsider going to lunch. But Tora's inner voice was louder. '*No lunch! Go inside and work off some of that fat you saw staring back at you in the mirror today, Tora Bora!*'

Tora Bora, a nickname her older sister Courtney had given her for always wanting things to be right and by the book, had stuck with her to this day. As children, Tora's honesty annoyed Courtney. She found her sister too righteous for her liking, hence the name Tora Bora. In other words, Tora was boring.

Tora smiled. "I know," then shut the car door.

Making her way up the bricked walkway, Tora turned and waved to Kate, who was once again admiring her tree. When she suddenly sped off, Tora went inside.

Kate seemed a bit odd today. Come to think of it, Kate had been acting odd for a few months now. Tora's over thinking sometimes caused her to make up scenarios in her mind, misconstruing what was really going on. She was trying to discipline herself to stop doing that and found distraction helped. Heading to her bedroom with only one thing on her mind, Tora kicked off her sneakers and walked to her mirrored closet.

Seeing herself in the mirror, Tora pointed to her reflection with determination, "You got this!"

Chapter

2

Sitting alone at her dining room table, Tora poked her fork around tonight's dinner, a frozen meal comprised of watery potatoes and a brown wet substance the carton sold as a meatloaf. Looking down at it, she wondered if anyone knew that for sure.

This was not how she pictured marriage. By now, Tora had imagined having two children, maybe three. She envisioned a noisy home with a dog that hung around the dinner table waiting for handouts from their rambunctious sons, and a husband who came home for dinner.

She always liked the name Everette, but she wasn't sure if that would be a name for one of her children or their dog. Ethan, Elijah, and the name Evan were some other baby names she'd tossed around. Tora loved the letter E and how it looked when written in calligraphy. She was also fond of Erika, in case she had a girl, but what did any of it matter when she was sitting at home alone on a Thursday night.

It sounded cliché, but Tora knew her biological clock was ticking and ticking loudly. She felt angry at herself sometimes for not pushing the children issue with her husband more. But if Dane didn't want children, and she forced him, well, what kind of father would he be and how would it affect their marriage? It seemed the future would be Dane and Tora, together forever, alone.

With no one to cook dinner for, life seemed to have lost some of its purpose. The house was always spotless and uncomfortably silent. Sometimes the sounds coming from the television, when Tora tried to entertain herself, only made her feel lonelier.

Then there were the nights she even felt single. Did Dane have to work so much? Did he have to take so much time away from their relationship, time away from her?

'Bentley!' her inner voice cried out when at that moment she decided she wanted a dog as soon as possible.

If she would be home in this quiet, empty house, without children, and a husband who constantly worked, she needed a companion. She would talk to Dane when he came home and plan to go this weekend. They could make a day of it and visit the local rescue shelter in search of the perfect dog. Preferably one with blue eyes like her and Dane, and their non-future children.

Knowing her request would be nearly impossible at a shelter, she wouldn't be picky. The chances were, she would take any dog whose sad eyes silently begged, "Take ME!" But a girl could dream.

Now, having something to look forward to, she felt hopeful. Denying Tora her chance at motherhood at the present time, would he begrudge her getting a dog? Most likely he would.

When going to other people's homes, Dane would complain about smelling their animals, including those with the most immaculate of homes. Even if there were no signs of an animal anywhere, he would insist that he picked up the scent, making him repulsed. He insisted that he smelled wet fur just walking past pictures of any creatures that may be hanging on the wall. Soon there would be no further invitations to a man who claims your home smells.

While Tora thought her husband had an incredible sense of smell, their friends thought he used that as an excuse so his kindhearted wife wouldn't bring home any strays. Knowing him as well as they did, they were probably right.

A sudden loud knock at the front door caused Tora to jump almost clear out of her seat. "Shit!" she angrily hissed at first, then laughed at herself for her startled reaction. As she headed for the door, she could see a few blurry images, moving behind the stained glass. Then she heard a loud cackling she knew too well.

"It's the Three Amigas!" Donna's croaky voice announced as Tora's silhouette became visible as she neared the door.

"Let us in!" the women demanded.

"Not by the hairs on your chinny chin chins!" Tora joked before opening the door wide, allowing the ladies to traipse in.

"We heard Dane was working so Ali and I jumped in Kate's car and voila! Here we are!" Donna beamed, throwing her large motherly arms in the air.

"We aren't interrupting anything, are we?" Ali joked as she crept in looking around suspiciously. "Any naked men?" Making her way to the dining room, she set down a plain white box on the table.

Tora could see the grease slowly seeping through the cardboard. "Donuts," she grumbled, looking up at the ceiling. "I just did a great workout and made a promise to myself to eat better."

"I see that from your healthy dinner," Kate replied. Crinkling her freckled nose, she looked down at Tora's meatless meatloaf as it slowly curdled in its cardboard tray. "What the hell is that, anyway?"

"Meatloaf."

"Looks like crappola." Kate murmured.

"You worked out," Donna reminded her. "You will continue burning calories all night now. Eat a donut," she said, flipping open the box top. "We have your favorite!" she temptingly teased in a singsong fashion, "Blue-berry cay-ake."

Blueberry cake donuts were Tora's favorite, but she couldn't help but wonder if this was another one of those private jokes shared between "The Three Amigas." It struck a nerve since Tora just referred to herself as a blueberry muffin at the clothing store with Kate earlier that day.

Stop looking for things to pick at, they are just being considerate.

"She is such a bad influence," Ali giggled.

As the ladies took their usual seats, Tora walked into the kitchen. "Tea? Coffee?" she asked, taking mugs out from the cabinet.

"Keurig?" Kate suggested, referring to the automatic single serve coffee brewer she had gifted to Tora last Christmas. Maybe Kate suggested it as a gentle reminder that she had bought it, but Tora loved the convenience and the gesture, so she didn't care.

"I can do that," Tora smiled eagerly, happy to oblige. Taking a box of coffee pods from overhead, she filled the water reservoir and slipped the first pod into the basket.

"Me too," Donna second.

"Me three," Ali smiled, raising her hand childlike.

While the coffee dripped, Tora grabbed the milk, sugar, and a few spoons. She laid them out on the table for the women as they sat hovering over the box of colorful donuts like a pack of hungry animals.

Tora handed out each mug full of coffee one by one and finally joined her friends at the table. "Well, this was a nice surprise," she smiled, lifting her personal blueberry cake donut out of the box.

"We didn't want you to be home alone," Donna smirked with what appeared to be an evil satisfaction to see Tora lift the cakey donut to her lips. "I was home alone too. Why should we be alone when we can be all alone together." she said, watching Tora take that first bite.

"Yeah, eating donuts!" Ali howled.

It was nights like this, when everyone could come together as one. In a show of their support for a friend, these were the special moments that cancelled out other times where Tora felt out of the loop, or like she didn't quite fit in.

It came easy to the others who were from the same town, knew the same people, heard and told the same jokes, shared memories, and practically lived the same life.

A more socially adept person could easily slide their way into any of the conversations between these women, but not

Tora. She didn't know how. Especially when feeling purposely pushed out.

Sitting with these ladies, laughing, reminiscing, drinking coffee and eating donuts, Tora's mind was temporarily free of the less than fun times they had shared in the past. Moments that seemed like a never-ending initiation period that left her feeling constantly judged.

This group of friends and their shared lives seemed to stunt their growth, much like the women who cherished the 80s. Those who wanted to relive what they would call, "the best years of their lives." As if outdated wardrobe and overdone hairdos could stop time.

It was the moments where Tora felt she picked up on private jokes or remarks by Donna, who could be a bully if she wanted, and she easily got away with it. No one had the nerve to call her out, especially at a difficult time in her own life when she pushed everyone to their limits.

Soon after Donna and her husband Scott separated, their only child, Scott Jr. gave his parents a run for their money. He was wild and aimless 'just like his mother' the ladies would joke; which Donna strangely took as a compliment.

Known to never worry, Donna did secretly worry. She was concerned for her son and his future, which prompted her to be at her most irritating and insulting. She wore her fear and sadness like a suit of armor, and quick as a wink, had the ability to verbally attack anyone in her company, including her friends when the mood struck.

Ali, Donna's closest friend, seemed to be her biggest target. The sweetest and most easygoing in the group, Ali made it easy for Donna to belittle her. It was tough to watch Ali struggle to hold back her tears. Tora and Kate would come to their friend's rescue by turning Donna's attention to one of her favorite subjects, *herself*.

It made everyone feel uneasy when witnessing Donna's cruelty firsthand. It embarrassed them for Ali because she didn't have the strength or knowledge to fight back.

They were all relieved when Scott Jr. matured and finally seemed to get it together after hopping on board his father's landscaping business. Donna eased up on everyone, including Ali. Yet no matter how hard Donna was on her, those two remained the closest of the four. They would resume their friendship as if nothing ever happened, and Donna never apologized or seemed remorseful.

Refilling everyone's mugs one by one and adding more water to the Keurig, Tora listened as Donna told her latest story of the most recent argument she had, and she'd had many. This one described a showdown, she'd had at the supermarket checkout, with the woman ahead of her who nitpicked every price, holding up the line.

"I told her, move it, lady! I ain't got all day!" Donna's booming voice and over the top gestures made her stories as interesting as they were exaggerated. Her performances could include acting out the scene, getting handsy, and using her friends as props. Donna wouldn't hesitate poking one of them in the chest or yanking an arm if it added to the story or if she felt she were losing their attention.

Tora chose to listen and observe as she refilled the mugs, handing them back again, one by one. While she appreciated her friends and their thoughtfulness, she could not help but think about that invisible wall that at times separated them, making her feel different. But tonight, that wall was down.

Would this be a good time to bring up what bothered her? While her head kept telling her how petty it was, her heart kept reminding her how much it hurt.

It made Tora feel isolated when the group referred to themselves as "The Three Amigas," like Donna did at the door tonight. There were four of them now, yet they still referred to each other as three. Why couldn't they change it to "The Four Amigas" she often wondered. Maybe not as catchy, but at least she would be included.

She would suggest it one night; a night she wouldn't mind being laughed at. Not tonight though. Tonight, it just felt good to connect over coffee and donuts. She felt like one of the girls. One of *these* girls.

Chapter

3

O h, what did you do? Tora scolded herself as she opened her tired eyes. Squinting through the ray of light that beamed inside of her room like a death laser. The fun was over, and now she was paying the price. All that coffee she drank last night made it hard to sleep when she finally laid her head on the pillow.

Today's plan was to get some work done. There were lists to make, welcome letters to the students that needed to be written and mailed; supplies that she needed to shop for. Her duties went on and on. Spoiled from sleeping late all summer, Tora found rising at the crack of dawn for the past few mornings to get on a schedule were hell, especially this morning.

Luckily, it was Friday, and that meant the next two days were for Dane and her to spend some much-needed alone time together, and to visit the local shelters to find a dog. With that thought, her cell phone began vibrating alongside her to-do-list of clutter that lay on the nightstand beside her bed. Organization was next on her list.

Sitting up in bed, she clumsily juggled the phone to her ear. "Hello?"

"Hey babe, can you hear me?" Dane yelled out over what sounded like bulldozers in the background.

"Yes!" she yelled back, rubbing her eyes.

"I'm so sorry. I will be working late again tonight."

Throwing herself back onto her fluffy pillow, her heart sank. "Again? It's Friday, Dane."

"I know. I know. What can I do? I'll be home as early as I can tomorrow. Before the sun comes up. I promise. I'll take you to breakfast at Flap Jacks." He knew how much she loved that place for their homemade Belgian Waffles.

Just what she needed, waffles, butter, and more sugar. She could tell her husband they didn't need the money that bad and he should just come home. On the other hand, he was trying to start up a business, and that took time, money and contacts. This was his dream, and you didn't want to rub people the wrong way so early out of the gate, but how much more time away from home could he possibly need?

Tora had grown tired of playing the supportive wife for a while now. She cheered him on, pretended everything was okay, but inside she felt neglected.

"OK, Dane," she said finally.

"I can hardly hear you! I'll call you later!"

Hearing the line go silent without as much as a goodbye, Tora just wanted to cry. The tone in her husband's voice and the length of today's call left her with an uncomfortable feeling. Her marriage was changing, and so was her husband.

With Dane out last night, Tora was able to tackle most of her to do list. Now it was Saturday, Tora and Dane's Day. Taking a break from her early morning practices of getting up with the roosters, it felt good to lay in bed without hearing an alarm. She couldn't wait to eat breakfast at Flapjacks and reconnect with her hard-working husband.

Thinking about what she would order, Tora knew she most likely would order the Belgian Waffles anyway. What was a date day without some sugar? Then, she began to feel bad for feeling bad. After all, her husband was trying to provide a better life for his wife. Dane was trying to start a business that could be handed down to their children and their children's children. He had the right intentions, but she couldn't help feeling angry sometimes, which in turn made her feel guilty.

Knowing she could get passed it, she outstretched her arm to Dane's side of the bed. It felt cold. Opening her eyes, Tora expected to see him there resting beside her, but he wasn't.

Seeing the television was still on and showing the Netflix logo was a telltale sign, Dane hadn't come home after all. He would have reprimanded her for falling asleep with the television on if he'd come to check on her like he usually did after not seeing her for days at a time.

Tora sat up and checked her cell phone on the nightstand beside her. It was 9 a.m. There were no missed calls and no texts. Although everything seemed a little off lately, this was more off than usual.

Untangling her legs from the blanket, she climbed out of bed and called his cell. It went straight to voice mail. Pacing the floor with worry, the cell phone in her hand began to ring. Without hesitation, she answered it. "Dane!"

"No, it's me Kate. Everything ok?"

"No, … uh, … yeah, … uh, … I don't know. Dane told me he would call me last night; he never did. He promised he would be home early this morning, but he isn't here."

"Did you call his cell?"

What a stupid question, Tora thought to herself. *Of course, I called his cell!*

"Yes, but it went to voicemail. I thought this was him calling now. I'm getting nervous, Kate."

"I bet everything is fine. Do you know what hotel he stays at? Can you call?"

"No. I never asked, and he never told me." Tora admitted, realizing how foolish that sounded after saying it. What if there were an emergency, just like today?

"Call his job. See if anyone can reach him and I'll tell Tom to try too."

"That's a great idea!" Tora said, moving her pacing to the living room.

"I'm stopping for coffee. I'll be right over."

"Thanks Kate."

Scrolling through the contacts in her cell phone, Tora searched for the number to the trailer. Tora and Dane had always spoken with each other on their cell phones, so she hadn't called the office in years.

What if he had an accident? What if he had a heart attack in the middle of the night, or what if he slipped and fell in the shower? He could have hit his head and was bleeding to death. Who would know? He was alone. Well, he may be with Sam, but Tora knew her husband. Dane had his habits, and he valued his privacy, making it doubtful they shared a room.

Catching herself in her old habit of over thinking, which she knew would only make matters worse, Tora took a deep breath to calm herself down. Slower now, she skimmed through her contacts, paying close attention to every name she saw. Finding "Trailer," she pressed call. After a few rings, an answering machine picked up telling the caller the office opens at ten on Saturdays.

Checking the time on her cell phone, it was only nine fifteen. Forty-five minutes seemed more like forty-five hours, but she had no other choice than to wait.

"How could you not have the numbers to his job in case of an emergency!" she scolded herself. "Stupid Tora, very stupid of you!"

Fueled by anxiety, Tora tried calling his cell again, this time leaving a message after the beep. "Dane, please call me. I am really getting worried. If you can't call, please shoot me a quick text, just so I know you're all right." She begged before ending the call.

Maybe his cell phone was dead. Maybe he had no service. Maybe, maybe, maybe! Taking another deep breath, Tora slowly exhaled. There had to be a reasonable explanation for all of this, if the waiting didn't kill her first.

Now standing guard at her front window, Tora noticed it began to rain. Slowly at first, her eyes focused on each droplet as it softly hit the glass. She enjoyed watching the rain and found it soothing. It wasn't long before Kate's yellow Beetle pulled into the driveway breaking her out of her trance.

Running to the door, Tora flung it open for her friend to come in.

"Thank you for coming Kate," She greeted, closing the door behind her.

"Any word?"

"Nope. The trailer opens for business at ten. I have some time before I call there again."

Handing Tora her coffee, "Let's sit for a moment," Kate suggested and walked toward the dining room.

"I know that I'm probably getting all worked up for nothing," Tora acknowledged, sitting across from Kate at the table. She knew how quick she was to worry. "There is probably a very simple explanation."

"Yes," Kate agreed. "I bet there is."

Kate has always been the very cool, calm type. Tora often needed that to balance herself out.

"But it's the waiting. The not knowing." Tora sighed.

"Personally Tora, I think Dane is fine," Kate confidently stated in what seemed to come across as more a matter of fact.

Or was Kate worried too, and only telling Tora what she wanted to hear, just like she did with that horrible blueberry muffin of a dress. Whatever the reason, it was a trait Tora wouldn't mind having herself.

"You know, I haven't seen Dane for days," Tora uttered softly, feeling ashamed as she spoke those words.

Kate frowned.

"God forbid something really happened. I would be so mad at myself for letting him work instead of insisting he stay home. When he called me yesterday, that was the last straw. But at the same time, I want him to *want* to come home, not *make* him come home."

"First of all, you need to stop getting all worked up. Second, don't blame yourself," Kate comforted. "We both know worrying doesn't make things better; it only makes them worse. Besides, if anything had happened," she shrugged nonchalantly. "Someone would have reached out to you already. So, let's just say that's -"

"It's ten!" Tora exclaimed, stopping Kate, mid-sentence, paying no attention to a word she said. Hitting redial, Tora waited. Suddenly her sad eyes lit up. "Jose! It's Tora, Dane's wife!" she greeted, relieved to hear a real person on the other end of the line.

Jose knew Tora. He had been with the company for as long as Dane.

"Have you heard from Dane today? I can't reach him on his cell."

Kate sat quietly, sipping her coffee.

"OK, thank you," Tora said, putting the phone on speaker and laying it on the table. "He put me on hold," she informed Kate.

Nervously she tapped her fingertips on the table. She feared the worst, or nothing at all. "What would I do if anything happened to him?" she asked aloud, staring off into space.

While Tora filled her head with all the horrible possibilities, Kate mumbled something, but Tora was too far off in her own head to pay attention.

"If something happened," she continued, "I'm sure the police or the hotel would have contacted me."

Kate mumbled again. This time a little louder.

Lifting her head, she looked to Kate puzzled, then asked, "What?"

"I have to tell you …" Kate's words quickly falling out of her mouth.

"Miss Tora!" Jose's voice yelled over the cell phone.

Kate deflated in her seat.

Taking her phone off speaker, Tora placed it to her ear. "Yes, Jose?" she asked, followed by a pause, and then her mouth dropped open. "What hospital?"

Kate threw her head back in surprise.

"Thank you so much, Jose!" Tora rushed, abruptly ending the call.

"What happened!"

Tora sprang to her feet. "Dane was in a car accident, or a car hit him, … I'm not sure," shaking her head. "He's at Mercy Hospital," Tora explained, then ran off down the hall toward her bedroom.

Kate jumped up and followed closely behind. "Is he ok?"

"All he really has told me so far was that the hospital called the trailer. Dane didn't have his insurance card on him," Tora panted out of breath, stepping out of her pajama bottoms and squeezing herself into a pair of yoga pants.

"Should I go with you? I can drive."

"Oh my God, these pants are so tight," Tora moaned. Taking hold of the waistband, she gave them a good yank. "No, no, it's okay. He may not be able to have visitors. I could be there for hours. I'll let you know what's going on. I promise."

Running into the mudroom, Tora crammed her feet into a pair of sneakers lying in the corner. Grabbing her tote bag and raincoat from the hook, she wrapped herself in both and turned to Kate. Touching her arm, "Thank you," she said, then ran out into the rain.

Closing the door behind her, Kate also ran out and into the safety of her own car.

The sky was getting darker and a large black cloud loomed overhead. The moment Tora's hand touched the handle, a low rumble of thunder sounded in the distance and the sky opened.

Tora had no idea that another storm was soon headed her way.

Chapter

4

Feeling Dane's accident was a sign, a warning from the universe to slow down, Tora promised herself she would do everything in her power to convince her husband to start taking it easy. Not only was she feeling guilty for not insisting he come home last night, she blamed herself for what happened.

Life was too short and too precious to work yourself in the ground. Exposing yourself to all that could go wrong, it was only a matter of time before something did, and now it had.

As the rain began to let up from the brief downpour once again, Tora could safely pick up speed. The hospital was less than a ten-minute drive and she didn't have much further to go.

All Tora wanted was to wrap her arms around her husband and tell him she loved him. She was desperate to see him and hoped that he would be all right. He had to be. What would she ever do without him? A world without Dane was unimaginable.

Thinking of all the things they hadn't done, Tora tried to remain calm, but couldn't help but expect bad news. They had talked about going places and doing many things, like the Niagara Falls trip that never happened. She wanted to see these falls for herself. They had always struck her as romantic.

They also talked about going to see the Grand Canyon. Dane would joke about attempting to take a selfie over the canyon, only to fall right in. What a vacation that would be, he would laugh to an unamused Tora, who never found the humor in other's misfortunes, especially the fatal ones.

Then there was Disney World. A place she looked forward to taking their children one day. If anything happened to her husband, having a child would be further from her reach than ever before.

He had to be all right, she told herself as she pulled into the parking lot in search of an empty space. It was crowded today. The hospitals always were on the weekend.

The distance between the parking lot and the main entrance to Mercy Hospital was not an easy task. Surprised to find a parking spot so fast, Tora pulled in, shut off the engine and rolled out of her car.

Running, she jumped over puddles and stormed right through the ones she couldn't clear. Her concern right now was Dane. She knew he needed her and was probably wondering why she wasn't there by his side already.

Making it to the entrance, Tora staggered into the lobby. Her wet, stringy hair hung down over her face, the belt from her rain jacket was hanging lower on one side, and her pant legs looked as if she walked through the river to get there.

"Can I help you?" A tall, burly security guard asked, giving her the once over.

Trying to catch her breath, "My husband, … he was hit by a car, … or in a car accident." she panted.

"Take the elevator up one flight, you'll see the nurse's station on your left." he directed, pointing behind her.

"Thank you." her voice trailing off as she spun around to catch the open elevator door not far ahead.

Walking right in, she pressed the silver button stamped 1 and waited. Shaking her leg, Tora watched as the thick metal doors slowly closed.

Forming a puddle where she stood, the thought of being reunited with her husband soon calmed her. However, the fear of a devastating outcome still lingered.

"Ding," the elevator warned as it was ready to move. Giving off a gentle pounce of air between her feet and the floor, her ride transported her to her future. Their future.

Another soft ding from the elevator let her know she had arrived. As the doors opened, Tora was thrust into a loud, bright, chaotic environment that overstimulated her senses.

Voices faded in and out from the staff who were rushing around tending to what seemed like an over flux of patients. The screeching sound of wheels turning from the patient stretchers in need of a good oil, were like nails on a chalkboard, as they rolled up and down the hall. The beeping of monitors blended with moans and groans from patients in pain made Tora anxious.

Were any of those sounds coming from Dane?

Reluctantly stepping out of the elevator, Tora picked a direction and wandered aimlessly down the hall. Somehow, she found her way to a long white counter labeled Nurse's Station overhead. There were a group of women clad in white uniforms huddled behind it. Some were looking over charts, while others were setting up small carts with little plastic cups as another nurse dropped a rainbow of pills in each one.

"Hello," Tora spoke under her breath, barely able to muster up more than a whisper. Shivering from the cold breeze that blew through the corridor, she pushed her wet hair from her runny mascara stained eyes to get a better look to whom she was speaking. "Dane, … Dane McAllister," her voice quivered through her pale lips.

"He was just wheeled to x-ray, but he has a room," one nurse stated, looking up from behind a clipboard. "His companion is in there now waiting if you want to go in." She smiled from under her tortoise shell framed glasses.

"His companion?" she asked. "Oh, Sam," she remembered. Tora found comfort in hearing Dane wasn't alone after all. Finally, she would get to meet the man who worked side by side with her husband for so many nights.

"Yes," the nurse replied while rifling through the papers attached to it. "She is waiting if you care to join her."

Tora's face felt flush. Her insides hollowed out. Did she hear the nurse correctly? Was she speaking of the right Dane McAllister? Obviously, there was a mistake.

A look of concern crossed the nurse's face. "Are you all right?"

"What room?" Tora asked, fighting to keep her composure.

"Are you all right miss?" the nurse asked again, a little louder this time.

"What room!" Tora demanded.

Pursing her lips, "Two twelve. Down the hall and to your right," the nurse answered, burying her head back down into the chart.

Making her way down the hall, Tora's legs felt like rubber bands. She struggled to find the strength just to stay on her feet.

It crossed her mind to turn right around and pretend as if she were never there. She could tell her friends her car broke down, or when she arrived Dane was in x-ray and they wouldn't let her in. There were a million excuses she could have used not to face this moment. This moment that could change her life forever.

Reading the numbers on the doors as she crept down the hall, Tora stopped within an inch of her husband's room. The door was open, but she hesitated.

Not sure if it was the frigid hospital or her nerves, Tora began to tremble. Running her cold, pruned hands along her wet face, she smoothed her hair and adjusted her raincoat.

This was it. She could never change who and what was awaiting her. Closing her eyes, she took a deep breath. Slowing exhaling, she opened her eyes and silently entered the room, saying a little prayer that the nurse had made a mistake.

A shapely, tall brunette stood by a large window with her back to the door. She couldn't see her face, but Tora sensed she would be pretty. Maybe even beautiful. Her long, thick, wavy brown hair cascaded down the middle of her back; it was shiny. Wearing snug fitting blue jeans and a fuzzy white sweater, she seemed well taken care of.

It wasn't too late. Tora could turn around and leave just as she came, but she was better than that. She could never stay in her marriage while secretly knowing about an affair. Everyone would pity her. Everyone probably already did. Poor Tora Bora.

If she wanted, she could sneak up behind this woman and give her one good shove, breaking out the glass, and fall face first on a car in the parking lot. That would be the quickest and easiest way to remove this thorn from her side. Tora could now understand what a crime of passion really meant.

Where would the sense be in that though? Sure, she would be rid of her, but was Tora willing to go to prison and lose her freedom for her cheat of a husband? The glass looked thick anyway.

If only she would turn around, she thought to herself, wanting to see her face. *No!* Realizing she didn't want to see her face. She didn't want this woman's image branded in her mind, making it too easy to imagine her and him together, every night as Tora pictured crying herself to sleep.

Her anger toward this woman switched over to anger toward Dane. He was to blame, not her. How long had this been going on? The lies, the stories about working late … working late? He wasn't even working!

She needed to think and fast. The last thing she wanted was Dane to return from his x-ray and see her standing there like some stalker. Tora was running out of time, she had to decide.

Just then, Tora began to hear light sobs coming from the woman. Her back hunching over with each exhale of breath. Raising her hands to her face, she wiped the tears from her cheeks. Rubbing her wet fingers together, she turned. Their eyes met. The woman's lips parted as if to speak, but nothing came out.

Seeing this woman's porcelain tear stained skin made it all too real for Tora. Now she had a face; a very attractive one at that.

Tora was sharing her husband with another woman, with this woman, and it sickened her to the core. Dinners with Sam while Tora ate alone. Making plans with Sam while Tora sat at home waiting. Hotel rooms with Sam; sex with Sam ... Sam, Sam, Sam, Sam, Sam!

There must have been trips, gifts, money, all while Tora was trying to watch every penny, doing without, just to help her husband sock away any extra for their future, really spending it on Sam. Now, here she was in the flesh and looking expensive to boot.

Tora could feel the pounding of her own heart almost to the point of hearing it. Could Sam hear it? Tora was on the verge of a collapse from stress and weakness. Could Sam see this?

It was the perfect opportunity to charge at Tora, knock her down to the floor, where she would undoubtedly fold up into a wet, mangled heap for Sam could make her getaway. But it was clear Sam was in too much shock to read Tora, even with the look of disillusionment written all over her face.

Time seemed to have slowed down. Seconds passed like minutes. Dane could be back at any moment, then what? Tora would then be faced with them both.

How would he react? Would he be speechless himself being caught between his wife and his girlfriend? Who would he choose, or worse yet, would he reprimand Tora for showing up at the hospital unannounced and console his traumatized girlfriend? As absurd as that thought had seemed, she found herself here today, which made the absurd extremely possible.

Nothing was hers. Not her marriage, their vows, the promises, nor their future. Her only concern now was to get out of there. With nothing to say, nothing to do, Tora slowly turned to face the door. She wanted to just leave, just disappear, so she did.

Beaten down, Tora dragged her feet along, too weak to lift them, and headed down the corridor back toward the elevator. Suddenly she became lightheaded. Feeling woozy, she leaned her back against the wall for support. She braced herself, trying to swallow as her throat tightened, a rush of nausea swept over her. Knowing she had to hold on, she refused to give them the satisfaction. She had to keep it together, at least until she made it back to her car.

Another cool breeze blew through the corridor, helping to clear her head, just enough to keep going. Hearing the ding of the elevator, she peeled her limp body from the wall. The doors slowly opened, and Tora shuffled in. Pressing L for lobby, the doors eventually sealed shut. Feeling that same gentle pounce of air beneath her, she waited.

All Tora could see during her ride back downstairs was Sam's face. It was etched in her brain. Her healthy long hair; perfect skin; green eyes framed by long brown lashes, and her body, it was fit, and that may have been what bothered Tora the most. Her slim figure and how well she wore her clothes served as just another reminder for Tora of how imperfect she was. It looked as if Sam took pride in herself. Something Tora hadn't done in quite some time.

The elevator doors opened. Stepping out onto the shiny waxed floor, Tora was back in the quiet lobby that just moments ago she couldn't wait to reach. Passing the security guard once more, he lowered his lids, avoiding eye contact. Tora, who appeared despondent, walked by, looking as if she had just received the worst news of her life. Her sadness was that of a woman mourning the loss of her husband, and in a sense she was.

The rain was coming down even harder than before. Each drop beating down, pelting her as she gathered up any energy she had left to walk through the flooded, football field sized parking lot.

Tora trudged through every puddle, every pool of water in her path, as the heavy rain continued to add insult to injury. Tora was numb.

Finally, making it to the solitude of her car, she stood there fumbling with the buttons on her key fob until it beeped allowing her entry. Climbing inside, she closed the door behind her. Dazed, she sat motionless at the wheel. Then, a slow but steady stream of tears rolled down her cheeks.

Violently she began banging the steering wheel with the palms of her hands. Missing, she pounced on the horn, causing it to beep, only angering her more. Grasping the wheel firmly in her hands, she pulled on it repeatedly as her body rocked back and forth. Letting out a cry like that of a wounded animal, her chest heaved in and out, and the tears she'd held in for so long were now pouring out. Throwing herself back into her seat she let out a yell.

As her sadness quickly turned to anger, Tora considered going back inside. No patience to wait for the elevator, she imagined herself running up the stairwell as fast as she could with the sudden thrust of adrenaline pumping through her veins.

She envisioned herself storming into the room and grabbing Sam by the hair, but then what? Her vision went black. Tora needed to drive away before her irrational thoughts turned into irrational actions.

With no clue of what to do next, Tora started her car. Who should she call? Who could she tell? She headed for home, but only out of habit. Once she got there, what would she do then? Make tea?

Emotions came in waves every few seconds. Sadness that her marriage was over, followed by rage toward Dane, jealousy toward Sam. The humiliation, the lack of respect. The audacity for Dane to have his girlfriend by his side instead of his wife was unbearable.

Then she began to question her own thoughts and what she had just seen. Could she be overreacting, was her overthinking at it again. Were they just coworkers? For a second Tora had a reprieve. As much as she would have liked to believe it was all just one big misunderstanding, she would never forget the paralyzing look on Sam's face. That right there said it all.

As she drove, her mind began to sort through the recent days. Dane's calls were brief and vague. He used to tell her he missed her, how he couldn't wait to get home to her, but he had stopped saying that.

Then she thought of Kate. Tora remembered Kate had called her earlier that morning, she didn't know why, and there was the strangeness Kate displayed after dropping her off home from shopping the other day. The odd reassuring of their friendship.

Tora had to call her. Give her an update. Not on Dane's accident, but his affair. She wanted to let her friend know she didn't have to hide it from her anymore. *What a relief that should be for Kate,* she laughed ironically to herself.

Clicking the voice button on her steering wheel Tora instructed, "Call Kate," through her car's blue tooth.

"Calling Kate," her blue tooth female voice responded.

Going straight to voicemail, "Hi, this is Kate. Please leave a message." her friend's chipper recorded voice stated.

Why didn't she answer? Wasn't she waiting to hear from Tora about Dane? Disconnecting the call, Tora didn't leave a message. She figured they all probably knew exactly what happened. Thick as thieves.

Making it home, with no recollection of how she got there, she pulled into the driveway. Shutting off her car, she sat there for a moment, fixing her gaze upon her precious Smoke Tree.

Then the rain began to let up. The last few drops of rain hit Tora's windshield. The sun's rays sliced through the clouds, absorbing them into the light. It was going to be a very clear day.

Chapter

5

Her birthday had since come and gone. There was no card, no flowers, not even a text from her cheating bastard of a husband. Was she expecting something? Anything? Yes, an apology. Just out of sheer human decency, spousal courtesy perhaps? Instead, everyone was going along with their business like nothing happened, including Dane.

Tora was sure he had forgot. Busy with his girlfriend, his wife's birthday just wasn't as important. The thought of that was not only crushing; it was insufferable.

Her sister Courtney called, wishing her the best day ever as she rambled on about the perks of being single. Her mother, Marie called from New York, they chatted briefly about taking some time off from work and visit her in the Big Apple, then rushed her off the phone to head out to the casino with her latest male companion.

Her friends, Ali, Donna, and to her surprise even Kate sent a text. They even toyed with the idea of doing something to celebrate, but nothing transpired. She hoped for someone, anyone to come banging at her door last night to drag her out on the town for a night of drinks and debauchery. No one did, and she couldn't blame them.

Tora knew she was miserable. How do you celebrate miserable? It's much like trying to light wet matches - you can't.

Stretching out from under her blanket, Tora turned to look over to Dane's side of the bed. Often waking in the middle of the night, she would imagine him lying there, beside her, fast asleep with his back to her, as if it were all a bad dream. That would be the best birthday present ever.

Replaying that day over and over in her head this morning, like self-torture, she kept asking herself if that was all? Walking away seemed so easy. Easy for Dane, easy for Sam, it was even easy for her, but was it weak? Should she have done something? Anything? Should she have fought for her marriage perhaps? How did other women handle these types of situations? Had any of them quietly walked away like she did?

While some would say it took a lot of strength to handle things the way Tora did, there weren't many women able to hand their man over so willingly. People fight for what they believe in, but there wasn't much to believe in that day.

Even if Dane reached out, which he hadn't, apologized, which he hadn't, begged on his hands and knees for forgiveness, he hadn't done that either, but if he did, how would she ever be able to trust him again?

Tora would have to pull it together since her new little army of third graders would invade her classroom soon. She could not bring her troubles there. Not only would it be unfair to the kids, but if they homed in on that weakness, boy would she be in trouble.

Teaching kids could be tough, especially if you did not have your shit together, and right now, Tora did not have her shit together. Past students could really give a teacher a run for their money; even an eight-year-old could wear you to the bit. As much as Tora loved children, and truly found a calling to teach them, there was no doubt she would have to find a stick to bite down on for the first few weeks.

Tora would return to work as a single woman now. What would she tell her peers when they asked what she did over the summer? What would she say when asked how Dane was doing? She knew it would shock everyone. Just as it had shocked her.

Before the beginning of the end of their marriage, Tora and her husband were the envy of other couples who were so sick of each other they couldn't help but wonder how Tora and Dane kept it together. They both appeared to still enjoy each other's company with laughter and public displays of affection.

She didn't know it then, but other couples had found their supposed happiness threatening, as it reminded them of the thread their marriages were clinging to. Then, once they separated, everyone scattered as if she had some sort of contagious disease they didn't want to catch.

If it hadn't been for that accident, how long would it have gone on? How many nights would she have wished her husband a 'good night' and to 'have fun' when he called to say he had to work late with Sam?

Tora would replay those cringe worthy phone conversations over and over in her head. She felt like such a fool. Dane must have felt like a slick genius.

Her mind had the ability to constantly taunt her with thoughts of Dane and his girlfriend. She created images in her head of the two of them enjoying glasses of wine, laughing, canoodling, their perfect bodies half naked, celebrating. Toasting not only to Tora's loyalty and trust, but her stupidity for her faith in a husband who was calling out sick to his marriage, so he could enjoy the freedom he was relishing with his girlfriend.

Would these feelings and these thoughts ever go away? She had her moments. Some days she felt she could handle it, and things were looking up to the point she seemed to be on the mend. Then there were the other days. Days she would flip through her phone, come across a picture or hear a song in her car, and she would just lose it. It felt like death, but even with death, there comes a time to move on.

Having no idea what time it was, Tora had to stop feeling sorry for herself and prepare to meet Ali. Distraction was her therapy. Since the breakup, Tora had seen less and less of her friends, especially Kate. Throwing herself into work, she appreciated the solitude when getting her classroom together for the new semester. It kept her busy but come the weekend she needed another outlet.

Bike riding around the lake was something she would look forward to doing with Dane almost every Saturday. Going through the motion of getting dressed and having to pull the bike out of the shed by herself seemed dismal and lonely compared to the way she remembered it with Dane.

Hopping out of bed, Tora would grab the water bottles while Dane could be heard in the backyard sliding open the squeaky doors to the rusted shed where they kept their bikes.

"Lettttt's riiiide!" he would joke with a devilish look in his eye, as if they were riding motorcycles instead of mountain bikes. He was so handsome, so charismatic, so fun.

After riding a while, her and Dane would stop at one of their favorite benches facing the lake and sit quietly. Staring out at the water, they would reflect on their life together. What they were building, and how lucky and grateful they were.

Grateful for waking, grateful for riding, and grateful for each other.

Now, Tora would take her own bike out of the shed and ride alone to the end of the block where she would meet Ali instead. Appreciating what her friend was trying to do, Tora couldn't help but feel it was out of pity or obligation. Tora's frame of mind needed to change if she was ever to get over this very large bump in the road, or was it a pothole? Either way, she knew she had to get over it.

"Get back on that damn horse!" she could hear her grandmother's voice instructing a young Tora during her summer visits to North Carolina. Tora, who literally would fall off the horse, persevered with her grandmother's encouragement. It was a small horse, but a horse all the same. That advice came in handy now as she needed to get back on that damn horse!

It would be the familiar situations in her life, such as bike riding by the lake, that were a constant reminder of how things that once were, would never be again. It was sad. She was pretty sure Dane was not lying around pining for her. She knew she had to get over it, but how? Everything she did, everyone she knew, brought her right back to him.

She forced herself to climb from beneath the safety of her blanket, out into her cold, lonely room. Closing her eyes tightly, she lifted her arms for a good stretch and let out a loud yawn. Opening her heavy, tired eyes, Tora found her reflection looking back in the mirror.

Her tousled long blonde hair hung down, obstructing the view of the chunkiness she was covering up under the security of her comfy gray sweats and a white tee. Tora had gained even more weight since that blueberry muffin of a dress fiasco. She could feel it was slowing her down, making things hurt that never hurt before.

Was this the disaster Dane saw every morning? *No wonder he found a girlfriend.* She looked nothing like that fit, put together woman she saw that morning in the hospital.

Thinking about Sam, the woman who brazenly had an affair with a married man, her married man, Tora felt an odd admiration for her. Maybe it was her ability to maintain her coiffed look that torrential rainy morning while Tora stood there dripping like a wet rat that had just crawled out of the sewer; or how effortless it was on Sam's part to make Dane, her loving husband, lie and cheat on someone as loyal and committed as herself. *It must have been the sex.*

"Enough!" her inner voice roared. She slid one mirrored door into the other, no longer being able to see herself. She pushed her hanging blonde hair to the side and began the battle of finding something, anything, to wear today.

Digging right in, she roughly slid the hangers along the rod, pushing each unwearable item out of the way in disgust.

Every article of clothing reminded her of something, whether it be her recent weight gain, or outdated fashions she wore for special nights out with Dane. The options were either too tight, too short, or too ugly, but then, there it was. Peeking out from between two drab gray blouses was a piece that made her stop and take notice.

Delicately lifting the hanger from the rod, Tora carefully slipped out a colorful floor-length skirt. It was a simple polyester skirt she had gotten for five dollars on the sale rack one day but treated it like it'd been spun from some fine silk.

When Tora would come across this skirt in her closet with the price tag still attached, she would pat herself on the back for the killing she had made. Then that little voice in the back of her mind would remind her: *It's not really a sale if you don't wear it.*

Smiling, her eyes fixed on the narrow skirt, admiring the splashes of color that vibrantly ran through it. Even when she picked it up three years ago, it was a size or two smaller than she was. Making a promise to herself to one day slither into it, specifically for that cruise her and Dane had talked about taking for their ten-year wedding anniversary, she held on to it. After all, just like her marriage at the time, it was perfect!

Today it represented yet another thing that would never be. Losing weight; that skirt; the cruise; all a waste of time, all waste of money, just like her marriage. Still, she refused to get rid of it.

Suddenly that voice in her head came back to remind her once again: *It's not really a sale if you don't wear it.* She wanted to yell back, "Shut up!" But Tora knew that little voice inside of her was right. Back in that crowded closet the skirt went.

Then, just for a moment, to amuse herself, she playfully considered slipping on that skirt to go riding. The thought of pulling that skirt over her chubby body made her laugh inside. All that changed when she pictured the vibrant pattern stretched out across her chunky butt, expanding the print, and thinning out the material.

More irritated than before, Tora continued to push and pull hangers violently across the rod as if she wanted to rip the clothing inside apart with her bare hands. How would she ever fit into a skirt that never fit her to begin with when her daily wear was slowly splitting at the seams, including her old reliable Fat Pants?

Most women had a pair. Fat Pants were a girl's go to pant. The purpose of this article of clothing was to make the wearer feel comfortable when bloated or having gained a few extra pounds. Since having passed that mark, she now had to resort to another fashion term she herself coined "Fatter Pants."

In jest, marketing this idea would cross her mind. It lifted her mood a little finding the humor in this sad predicament she swore she would never be in. While women would purposely purchase and openly use the term *Fat Pants*, would women buy and wear *Fatter Pants?* She didn't think so. But it was her sense of humor that pulled her out of the dismal places her mind had often gone to lately.

Tops were also an issue lately as they rolled up over her rounded belly, while her ever shrinking pants slid down around her hips, leaving her midsection exposed if she didn't pull and tug throughout the day. What she really needed was a good pair of suspenders.

"Too tight," she moaned, pushing yet another hanger to the right, "Too short, … Too long, … Oh my god I'm so fat!" she spat, yanking the clothes from their hangers causing them to fall onto the closet floor as a result of her tantrum. Who knew getting ready for a bike ride would be so stressful?

This could not have been a better time than to pull out all the unwearable items from her closet, which was almost everything, bag them up and ride her bike straight to the local Good Will for someone who truly needed clothing. Stubbornly and selfishly she refused.

It may have been a closet full of misfits, but they were her misfits. Deep down, she couldn't part with most, if any, of the crap that hung in her closet, especially that skirt. Having promised herself she would wear that skirt, she would go on that cruise, and take pictures to post all over social media to rub in her ex's face, in the closet the skirt would remain. She didn't need Dane to take a cruise. She didn't need Dane to wear that skirt. All she needed was to lose some weight. *One day*, she vowed. O*ne day*.

Chapter

6

The air was crisp. Summer was taking its last breaths before Autumn would officially take over. It was a perfect day for a bike ride around the lake, and the two friends rode together, soaking it all in.

"I needed this!" Ali called out to Tora, who was trailing a foot or so behind her.

"You needed this?" Tora said under her breath.

Having a true appreciation for living in a state that had four seasons, Tora could not understand how some would want the same weather year-round. Sure, the warmer weather was nice with more to see, more to do, but wasn't it lovely to have one season end to witness the beauty of another begin.

The first snowfall; a dewy spring rain; the salty sea air mixed with suntan lotion as the hot sun warms the body. Jumping in a pile of leaves and hearing them crunch. Those are the sights, sounds and smells that awaken the senses. Things taken for granted that are gifted to us each day.

Weather could also have a way of bringing you back to your childhood, when the biggest problem in life was failing a test, or not getting the doll you had hoped for on Christmas.

The upcoming season gave us the warm, rich colors signaling it was boots and jeans weather. *Sweater weather*, and Tora loved the comfy, snug feeling that came along with it.

"Ring-a-ling, Ring-a-ling." The sound of Ali's bike bell would sound off at every flip of her thumb, alerting those ahead someone was riding up behind them.

While most knew to let bikes pass on the left, others who were not familiar with the protocol would become startled when hearing a bell. It could be wickedly entertaining to see the people ahead nervously shuffle from side to side in fear of being mowed down.

Now riding for almost thirty minutes, they both found themselves losing steam.

"Let's sit," Ali called out over her shoulder, leading them toward the benches overlooking the lake.

"I'm so thirsty," a sweaty Tora panted, pulling her bike up alongside Ali's. "I feel so out of shape." Lifting her water bottle from its holder on her bike frame, she took a long sip.

Together they sat side by side taking in the lakes' amazing view. Reflections of the trees mirrored into the water active with wildlife, creating a visually breathtaking display of nature's natural works of art.

"This is life for these creatures," Tora exhaled. It was relaxing to observe the water birds, all sharing space in this huge lake. "They all look so content."

Did these fine-feathered friends have the same issues people did? Did they argue, or step out on their main bird, and how in the hell could they even tell each other apart, when to her, each group of birds looked the same.

Was there a prettier one, a fitter one? Was there one that quacked too much or didn't quack enough? Was there a mean bird that would nip another bird in its feathered backside if it were moving too slow? *That would be the Donna bird*, Tora laughed to herself.

Starting to compare her own faulted relationship to that of these birds, she chided herself for once again letting everything and anything bring her back to thoughts of her dissolved marriage. Including sitting on the bench, trying to avoid the old, dried up bird droppings that lay splattered along the wooden slats, just as she had done in the past with Dane. Now, even poop was a reminder.

"So. How are you?" Ali puckered.

Tora could hear the sympathy in her friend's voice. She didn't like it. "I'm okay," she panted, sipping more water.

"We can still do something for your birthday. Girl's night out for dinner and a movie?"

"Nothing. That's what I want to do. I'm just glad it is over."

"If you change your mind, I know the girls are all in."

Tora smirked. "Kate? Kate's all in? I haven't seen her since everything happened with Dane."

Tora found it disheartening that out of their small group, Kate was the one most absent. Tora and Ali were the least close, yet here they were, riding bikes in the park together today.

"I can talk to Kate," Ali assured her.

"Don't!" Tora snapped. "Don't worry about it," she then quickly corrected herself, hearing the harshness in her tone. "My biggest problem, or what I should say, my biggest question is - what happened?" turning her body toward Ali.

"I rack my brain sometimes trying to recall a sign, any inclination Dane wasn't happy. I can't." She shrugged. "Then again, I didn't even have a clue he was cheating. Now, when I really think about things, it was so obvious," shaking her head. "He wasn't even coming home. That should have been a red flag right there."

When did it all start unraveling? Was it during a movie they were watching as they sat on the sofa in silence sharing a box of chocolates? Or was it the day at the beach when Dane seemed engrossed in texts from work, while Tora, in her usual blissful ignorance, kept busy by watching the paddle boarders, thinking about trying that herself one day.

Fully aware their sex life had slowed down, Tora chalked it up to all those late nights at work. Now, she could confirm that's exactly what it was, those late nights at work. She hated herself for not being more intuitive. She hated herself for being so stupid, so blind, and most of all for making it so easy. Tora trusted her husband. Should she fault herself for that? Was Dane faulting himself for what he did?

Turning to Tora, Ali sunk down in her body looking sad herself. "Sometimes men just don't feel good about themselves Tor, and some need a lot of attention. If someone takes an interest in them, it makes them feel good. It makes them feel wanted. It also shows their partner other people want them too. I read about it. It's like, *look at me. I still got it*," she mocked using a high pitched, exaggerated voice. Then she rolled her eyes. "Sometimes men like the thrill of the chase. It's fun, it's new." Ali said, looking up at the sky aimlessly as if cue cards were overhead, telling her what to say.

The words *fun and new* blazed through Tora's mind like a hot poker.

"I know this was not what you had planned. Maybe you can turn this around; make a bad ball good. Look at Donna, she's single and loving it."

Tora chuckled finding that statement downright out loud laughable. "I wouldn't exactly say she's loving it."

"She enjoys being alone." Ali insisted.

Tora arched her brows. "She does?"

"Donna says that all the time. She doesn't have to cook for anyone, she can come and go as she pleases."

"You believe that nonsense? I mean, if Donna found another man that she could tolerate, or rather a man that could tolerate her, I think she would get married again. She's always on those dating websites. She has like six memberships," she laughed, amused at the line of crap Donna fed Ali sometimes. Amused by the crap Ali believed.

Ali seemed to think about that for a moment, appearing to be taking Tora's reasoning into consideration. Just because Donna said she was happy being single didn't mean she was happy being single. As naïve as Tora felt she could be, she knew Ali had her beat.

"Well, I don't know about that, but what I do know is she and Scotty would still be together if Dane didn't slip."

"If Dane didn't slip? Slip about what?"

"If Dane didn't tell Scott he and Donna had a fling in college, I think those two would still be together. It didn't seem to bother you though."

Tora took an invisible punch to the gut. "It didn't bother *me* because I didn't know Dane and Donna had something in college. Are you sure?"

Ali wagged her head excessively, "I'm positive. Remember that year you had the flu and didn't make it to the Christmas Party? Dane and Scott got pretty shit faced and started one upping each other. Guess who won."

Thinking back, Tora remembered that night well. She was pleasantly surprised when Dane had come home earlier than usual. He said it was because she was feeling sick. He told her he'd come home to take care of her.

Tora was touched, and it only made her love him even more. Normally she would have had to drag him out of there if he didn't pass out on their host's sofa first. Dane was oddly quiet that night; preoccupied. Now it made sense.

"How long did that last, Donna and Dane?"

The "Three Amigas" rarely spoke ill of each other, nor did they reveal intimate details. Being alone with Ali, who seemed willing to share some inside information here on this bench, was probably a onetime only offer that Tora would milk.

"A few months," she said, tilting her head to the side, like it was no big deal. "Donna was hard to handle. A real handful and combative, mad all the time. Kind-of like she is now." Ali giggled. "I don't think Dane cared for that negative energy. It didn't fit with his persona either. Shortly after they broke up, Scott and Donna became engaged and got married."

Tora squinted her eyes. "So, Scott and Donna were dating when her and Dane hooked up?"

"I'm not sure of the details. You'll have to ask Donna."

Tora wasn't asking Donna anything, and how didn't *Ali* know the details? "They seem so, so, … opposite. Not each other's type at all."

"I guess at that age you don't really know what your type is. But she was popular in college. A lot of guys wanted to date her. Even the professors. Then she had kids and got - never mind! Don't tell her I said that! Or anything else for that matter!"

"Don't worry. I won't," she assured her frightened friend. Knowing how easy it was for Ali to be on Donna's shit list, Tora wasn't repeating any of what Ali had told her today or any day.

"Did you and Dane?" Tora asked, waving her finger toward Ali left and right.

Ali looked at Tora and let out a loud laugh. "Oh no, no, no. I didn't want her sloppy seconds."

Ali's remark gave Tora a bad taste in her mouth.

"Dane was a friend, and too much of a player for me," she continued, as if not knowing how offensive what she just said was. "Besides, I dug my claws into Vin." Ali beamed, referring to her own husband.

Tora admittingly found her husband to be a charmer. He was handsome and gifted with a great personality. He never came across as the *player type* to Tora, who just began to realize, she knew nothing about the man she married.

When Tora met Dane, it seemed their relationship was exclusive from day one. He was extremely attentive and always made himself available and always reachable. Except for Fridays. He reserved those nights for thanking the crew he led by taking them out for dinner and drinks.

Just then, Tora had an epiphany. Fridays were probably his cheat day back then, and as usual, she never suspected a thing. Just one more thing to add to the list of things she made so easy for him.

Looking out across the lake, Tora couldn't help but wonder what other deep dark secrets her husband had. There were times she felt things were a bit peculiar; she just couldn't put her finger on it.

Tora really had nothing to go on when it came to men. Having no brothers, her parents were divorced, and her father had since passed away. Now it all started to come together, as if someone lifted the blindfold.

"Are you all right Tor? You have to take care of yourself."

Tora knew she had to take care of herself. If she didn't, who would? Certainly not her husband, she knew that for sure. "I will be all right Ali. I just need some time to heal. I thought we would be together forever."

"What we think, what we see, it's not always the way it is."

"I know that now, and while it's still pretty fresh, I know it's over. It's not like I am waiting for him to come begging me for forgiveness so I can take him back with open arms."

Ali looked surprised, "So that's it? Kate says maybe you guys will get back together after Dane tires of this new thing he's got going."

Flaring her nostrils as if she had just smelled something bad, Tora was livid. Why would Kate even think such a thing! She was heartbroken not desperate!

"Is that what Kate would do? Would KATE take TOM back if he cheated and then tired of HIS new thing HE had going!"

"Kate misses you, Tora."

"Did she say that?"

"No. I just feel like she does."

"She doesn't even call me Ali. Once in a blue moon she shoots me a hello text when she seems to know I can't answer. Or, late at night when I'm asleep, just like she did for my birthday. She is avoiding me Al."

Tora understood she was very much the downer lately. Could it be she just expects too much? People had their own troubles, or maybe no one wanted to take sides.

One thing was for sure, Tora needed new outlets; a change of scenery, fresh faces to distance herself for a while. How was she ever going to have closure, find peace, when so many people, places and things, including her wardrobe, reminded her of her husband every single day? A support group crossed her mind. She needed other women she could talk to about lying, cheating husbands. There must be plenty out there. Finding them was another story.

"Wanna head back?" Tora asked.

Before Ali could reply, Tora was up and walking to her bike. She hid it well, but inside she was still furious. Why did it seem as if everyone was expecting her to sit by idly waiting for Dane to come back? It was as if he just needed to get something out of his system like the flu.

If someone would just say "His loss is your gain, or you are the best thing that ever happened to Dane and he will be one sorry man someday Tora," it would make a world of difference to her. It was simple. Why couldn't someone just figure it out?

This wasn't new to these women either. Remembering back to a time when Ali thought her husband Vincent was cheating, Tora was on the phone with her friend all hours of the night. Sometimes they would drive past her husband's job site to make sure he was where he should be and when.

Then there was Kate, who was having difficulty with her husband Tom's family, especially his sister Ruby. Again, Tora played the good friend. Tora would make Kate laugh by poking fun, mimicking and mocking Ruby to make light of the difficult process of fitting in with the in-laws.

And Donna, well, just putting up with her was supportive enough.

They all agreed it was the love and laughter they shared as friends that saw them through the tough times. Now that it was Tora's turn the past seemed to be forgotten.

It wasn't like Tora didn't understand the position the other ladies were in. She knew being friends with both her and Dane made it complicated, but wasn't there a girl code? Tora felt women should stick together. Where were *her* cheerleaders when she needed them? Where was Team Tora?

All those years of going with the flow for Dane, for these ladies, the efforts, the brushed off feelings, the work. With each turn of the pedal, each powerful thrust resulted in a sudden surge in speed as Ali was the one now struggling to keep up. It was as if Tora had a second wind, a fire from under her she was trying to surpass, all while burning more calories determined to fit into that closet full of shrinking clothing, and that skirt more than ever.

Silently and separately, they rode until coming upon Tora's block. Waving their goodbyes, Tora turned the corner and there she was, heading right toward her. The mysterious neighbor from around the corner - Rebecca.

Chapter

7

Rebecca was a celebrity in her own right. While the women didn't know her real name, Donna gave her that moniker one day when she saw her in the supermarket.

Overhearing another woman in the store saying how much the spandex clad blonde in the fruit aisle reminded her of that model turned actress Rebecca something or other, the name stuck. Her mere presence seemed to shake up everyone that day with their whispering and turned heads, including Donna who HATED women like her.

Radiating beauty and positive energy, Rebecca could be found using the neighborhood as her own personal gym. She oozed glamour and perfection in every step as if it were choreographed. Her tan and toned body, wearing her signature black racer back top with matching knee-length capris that hugged every curve of her defined hamstrings and well-rounded derriere, were something most women could only wish for.

Her bouncy ponytail and perky strut came straight out of a television commercial, and Rebecca was the star.

Now here she was in the flesh, only feet away, turning her golden mane toward Tora and flashing that smile.

To Tora, this woman represented power. Rebecca could stop traffic. Men loved her, and women wanted to be her, yet hating her at the same time. That included Tora's friends who would mock and imitate her any chance they had. But it meant nothing, because no one seemed to be happier than this fair-haired stranger.

"The Three Amigas" never walked or jogged, nor had they ever seen a gym, other than driving past one.

The funny thing was how her friends viewed other women who took the time to take care of themselves with instant dislike. They were a threat, a reminder of what eating right, and exercise could do.

Tora just admired her. She knew firsthand how tough other women could be on each other, especially her own friends.

It was Kate back then, who had kindly taken Tora under her wing and into the fold over a shared passion for entertainment trivia. Donna and Ali eventually came around, but not without a fight, especially from Donna, who could be tough on anyone new, tough on anyone period.

Happy in her marriage and in a younger, tighter body, Tora once gave off that same positive energy that people seemed drawn to. Her positive attitude toward life made others feel good and uncomfortable at the same time. Tora also had depth. With her own opinions and confident demeanor, she was interesting once.

Grabbing her water bottle, Tora headed for her squeaky shed to put her bike away before disappearing into her house.

Taking her usual position in front of her bay window, between sips of water and leg stretches she waited for Rebecca to pass again.

Placing her hands on her waist, Tora gave her soft sides a squeeze. Feeling the fleshy softness between her fingers, her face soured.

"Flab," she said aloud. "Flab, flab, flab." The more she said it the funnier it sounded. Determined to make changes, Tora turned to her worst enemy and headed straight for the mirrored closet in her bedroom.

Covered up with her signature ensemble, a loose-fitting tee shirt and baggy sweatpants, Tora felt she didn't look all that bad. Pulling up her t-shirt and tucking it under her chin exposing her soft white belly she gave it a slap.

"You are flabulous darling," she mocked in her fanciest voice, "simply flabtastic."

Then her eyes sharpened. Her smile turned down at the sides, "and this is why your clothes don't fit!"

Cupping her 36C, tan brassiere covered boobs she gave them a lift then let them drop. Surprised by the loss of height her breasts had taken over time, she realized there would be more changes she was not aware of.

Turning her back to face the mirror, Tora pulled down her sweatpants. She had no idea what was going on in back if she was unaware of what was going on right in front.

Peeking over her shoulder to get a look at the back of her thighs, she prepared herself for the worst.

Pressing her index finger into the crease between her butt cheek and thigh, she lifted the skin, smoothing out of the dimply, orange peel look it had. Letting it go then lifting it again, Tora could see the difference of what some firming up could do.

When did this happen? She never had cellulite. Even the slimmest of women had cellulite, but not Tora, until now.

Tora was picking herself apart. It was becoming a habit. Her husband's cheating was taking a serious toll. She felt unwanted, unloved and unattractive, but did she have to be so hard on herself?

Defeated and disgusted, she lifted her chin and her tee shirt dropped slowly like a curtain at the closing act of a terrible play. Bending over, grabbing the waistband of her sweatpants, she pulled them up and sat sulking on her bed.

What happened? The more weight she'd gained, the more she'd been covering up, and the less she had looked at herself in the mirror. Out of sight, out of mind.

Oh God, it's just too much work! It's double of me now. I'm not just Tora. I'm Tora times two. I'm Tora, Tora! Her insecurities cried out as anxiety and negativity began to swirl.

If you can't lose the weight Tora, Tora, why don't you just toss that skirt and go shop for Fatter Pants? Her taunting inner voice taking its turn to rear its ugly head.

The thought of shopping for new clothes, new larger clothes infuriated her.

No! It doesn't have to be like this Tora. You can fix this. You can make yourself look and feel better,' her positive inner voice fought back, motivating her. *'That's it! NO carbs, NO sugar! You rode today and will do something else tomorrow.'*

It was all about her frame of mind and what she wanted, and what she wanted was to feel less like Tora, Tora and more like Rebecca.

Chapter

8

Jumping out of bed, Tora was caught off guard as her legs buckled beneath her. Pained and sore from biking with Ali yesterday, she held on to the end of the footboard and pushed herself up. Straightening out, she smiled with satisfaction finding pleasure in almost collapsing to the floor in agony. No pain, no gain.

With stiffness in her step, she walked to her mirrored closet like a bow-legged cowboy. Looking at her pained body, she faced her biggest obstacle, herself.

"You got this girl!" she pointed to the woman staring back at her. Knowing what she wanted, all she needed now was the drive. Think it - believe it - and it will happen.

It was Sunday, and in the past this day was reserved for Brunch at Donna's where Tora and the other ladies would gather, get a late morning Mimosa buzz, while feasting on eggs, bacon and mini pastry. Tora missed this tradition that seemed to end once her and Dane broke up. Maybe it was for the best, she convinced herself, as this overindulgent day contributed to her weight gain over the years.

Sundays would now be strictly dedicated to taking care of Tora. Exercising, shopping to stock the fridge with healthy food, and getting ready for the workweek ahead was the plan. Tora had goals.

Heading to her living room, she stretched those sore muscles of hers. Taking her position in front of her window, she took hold of her ankle bending back her leg. Pulling her foot to her buttocks, Tora couldn't help but let out a moan while giving the front of her thigh a good stretch. She felt how tight and wound up her body really was. It hurt so good.

To pull it together for herself and no one else would be a challenge. Giving up was an option. Throwing in the towel was always the easiest, just like she did with her marriage, only this wasn't her marriage.

Could Dane, one man, finish her for good? With every fiber of her being, she would not let that happen. Dane had control over everything else in her life still to this day. He had the upper hand when it came to their friends and her living in their home, but he no longer had control of her.

At this point, Tora knew it wasn't about Dane anymore. It wasn't about the weight as much as it was about how the weight was making her feel. How the unhealthy food she was consuming, and the late-night snacking affected her overall health, which included her state of mind. Tora knew if she felt better, her outlook would be different, and that would help guide her toward independence. While she didn't expect to be a size two, she knew all she needed was a change.

Slowly beginning to do squats, she asked herself why she didn't get up and move when she just stared out the window every day? She could've multi tasked by burning calories slowly. Tightening, toning, and stretching, so she didn't feel so stiff when getting up out of a chair.

Just staring out of the window without some type of movement now seemed like a waste of time. Any calories burned were good calories. If she acted now, it would be a lot less work later in life and she would be ahead of the game.

Then from the corner of her eye, she spotted her, Rebecca. Did this woman ever sleep? Continuing her squats, determined to smooth out that cellulite, or at least try, Tora watched as Rebecca worked her magic.

Trotting proudly down the street like a show pony, Rebecca was on the move. Her toned bent arms pumping back and forth, legs rapidly taking her to her next level of fitness, she truly appeared a force to be reckoned with.

Tora's next item on her agenda would be talking to Rebecca. Walking up alongside her and striking up a conversation was at least something to consider. She always looked so friendly, so approachable. Maybe she could be a workout buddy. The worst thing she could say is no, or just laugh in her face, but Tora was willing to take that chance.

Hearing her cell phone ring, Tora followed the sound back to her bedroom and to her nightstand. Seven thirty a.m. her cell phone read and displayed "Sis calling." It was strange for Courtney to call so early, especially on a Sunday.

"Hey Court," she greeted into her cell phone. "Everything okay?"

"Hey, Tor." Courtney happily greeted back through what sounded like barking in the background.

"Is that a dog I hear?"

"Yes! That's Peanut! We just got her yesterday! She is the cutest Yorkie ever!" Courtney gushed over the phone.

Courtney's husband Benjamin had practically begged his wife for a dog, a German Shepard to be exact. He was reminiscent to that of a child nagging their parents for a pet, with promises to feed it and walk it. Today, she'd met him less than halfway with a dog named of all things *Peanut*.

Wondering how her brother-in-law put up with her high maintenance sister boggled Tora's mind. Ben was a good partner; always by his wife's side and forever loyal. He was much like the German Shepard he'd always wanted.

Maybe if Tora were more demanding and high maintenance like her sister, Dane would not have sought another woman. He wouldn't have had the time nor the energy.

"Wow." Tora laughed, "I never ever thought you would get a dog. Especially since you are never home."

"Well, that's why I'm calling."

Uh oh, here it comes.

"I have a small favor to ask. Benji and I want to drive out of town, spend a few days at the shore. I can't possibly take Peanut. I was wondering if you wouldn't mind watching her for me."

Tora highly doubted she could care for anything or anyone other than herself right now. The timing was awful.

Waking up today with a new attitude, and a plan, Tora was feeling renewed. It was as if something inside of her awoke. Not having turned to check Dane's side of the bed this morning, Tora was making progress. Did she have the time and the patience to be responsible for another living being, and would this small favor set her back?

"I have a lot going on, Court," she said, walking back to her living room window, preoccupied once again by the sight of Rebecca. Checking for any changes, Tora squeezed her butt cheek and scowled over its squishiness.

"You have nothing going on Tora Bora," her sister laughed condescendingly.

While Tora really didn't have anything going on, at the same time, she had everything going on. She felt as if someone had tossed her life into a blender and pressed start.

Calling her by the nickname Tora Bora wasn't getting her sister any brownie points either.

Sighing heavily, "Court, you just got the dog," Tora reminded her, shaking her head at her sister's lack of consideration for anyone, ever.

"Yesterday."

"And you're leaving her already," she snapped, walking away from the window, annoyed as Rebecca disappeared around the block again. This conversation alone was derailing her.

"Oh c-mon', just this one favor."

Favor was Courtney's middle name. Can you let my air condition guy in? Would you mind hanging around for my furniture delivery while I go get my hair done? I may have left my door unlocked, could you drive past the house and check? The requests were endless, but today, at this moment, in Courtney's mind it really was just this one small favor.

Marching back and forth, Tora thought to herself how she wished her sister would have children. It would brighten up Tora's life and she knew she would be the one watching them most of the time.

Living a childless life was disappointing, but this was the hand Tora was dealt. Now, without a husband, Tora knew she probably would never be a mom, but she could still be Aunt Tora.

It was sad, but Tora was at peace not having children with Dane. It would have been doubly hard to go through the disintegration of her marriage with children involved. Then she would have had to deal with Dane, and possibly his perfect and beautiful girlfriend regularly. That was only if he turned out to be a responsible parent.

She would see it for herself, every year with the different students, the children of divorce were suffering. In the end, her own children would have paid the price, and for Tora, that alone would be even more heartbreaking than not becoming a mother at all.

"In the time it took you to pick out a dog you could have had sex and maybe gotten pregnant," Tora said with a laugh, trying to lighten up her own mood.

"That is EXACTLY why I DO NOT have children Tora," she snapped. "I do not have the time to make them, and I certainly don't have the time to look after them. I don't even have time for this dog!" she snarled as Peanut began a new round of barking.

Poor Ben. Those two probably never have sex.

"Why don't you just pick it up!" Tora yelled, annoyed at her sister's lack of common sense and the constant yapping in the background.

Tora knew her sister didn't have patience, nor did she have maternal instincts. That included pets and even her own husband Ben. She honestly didn't think her sister would make a very attentive mother and would often chastise herself for suggesting it. She could see Courtney's children running around with the scissors or untied shoes if the nanny wasn't around.

"When are you leaving?" Tora sighed.

"Now."

"OK Court, I'm here."

"See you soon." she shot then abruptly ended the call.

As the older sister, Courtney was always the boss. At a young age she learned the art of manipulation once she saw the new baby, her little sister Victoria, getting all the attention.

Tora hadn't really thought about it, until recently, how no one ever seemed to care about what she thought or how she felt, even back then.

Their parents seemed to go along with this behavior by enabling Courtney. They gave into her demands, if only to avoid a big scene or dramatic public displays.

Courtney knew timing was everything. She'd become a professional.

Tora's grandmother filled the void, and when she passed away, it devastated Tora. Now, with their mother living in the city, it was just the two sisters, and that was a difficult relationship to maintain.

When vacationing together as couples if Courtney wanted to go to the more expensive resort or restaurant, the more frugal Tora would give in; mostly to avoid embarrassing her husband.

More expensive did not always mean better. Like the time they went to Primo Cuts, a high-end steak joint in the resort they were staying at. The outrageous price of the entrees, which were sub-par, and cocktails, which were not top shelf liquors, set Dane back a week's pay compared to Ben; a sports medicine doctor who probably earned that or more per patient.

Dane never made Tora feel she should accept less or argue over the cost of a dinner, or a vacation, no matter the impact on their bank account. It was as if whatever Tora wanted Dane made it happen.

Everything seemed to revolve around their marriage and Tora herself, so for Dane to cheat made it especially hard to understand. Dane made his wife feel like she was the only woman in the world for him, the only person who put her needs first, unlike her sister, unlike their parents, but exactly like her grandmother. She missed that; she missed them both.

'What would Rebecca do in this situation?

First, her husband walked over and out on her. Now her sister was about to do the same thing. She bet no one walked over and out on Rebecca.

Maybe her next time around, Tora would seize the moment and introduce herself. After all, it was a public area. Tora could run wherever she wanted, but would it make her seem needy? Would she be invading her space, her privacy?

Hearing the jingle of keys, Tora rushed to her front door and waited. Dane? Her heart raced. What could he want? Was he home begging for forgiveness?

Who cares! You're not taking him back.

As the door swung open, it was Courtney who waltzed in. Stopping midway, she took notice of Tora standing at attention.

"You look as if you just pooped your pants!"

Totally forgetting her sister had an emergency key, Tora couldn't help but feel self-conscious of how pathetic she must look to her sister. Standing there, expecting something else, someone else, maybe Dane.

Then she noticed the puppy resting in the crook of her sister's arm. Dressed in a tiny black sweater, a small pearl necklace and a diamond tiara secured to her little furry head, the movie Breakfast at Tiffany's came to mind, only for dogs.

Courtney, looking rather overdone herself, resembled a tourist with her wide-brimmed hat, large sunglasses and a yellow sundress. Tora couldn't tell which was more out there, the furry Hepburnish pooch or its outlandish owner.

"Here is my little Angel. Now, you be a good girl for your Auntie Tora."

"Is she wearing clothes?" Tora asked, awkwardly taking this tiny, fragile creature in her hands. "They're so small." she couldn't help but giggle. "Is she wearing doll clothes?" trying her best not to sound sarcastic.

"No!" Courtney bit back. "They're custom designed for her. I have her wardrobe right here."

Wardrobe? Tora watched in disbelief as her sister reached outside and pulled in Peanuts small pink suitcase, standing it in a corner of the mudroom.

"Where were you when you called, around the corner?" Tora half laughed, trying to comfortably position the little pup in her arm without disrupting her clothing and accessories.

"Yes. Yes, I was," she shamelessly admitted. "Here are her vittles," she said, placing the doggy bag on the floor. "A few treats and her favorite toy. Inside her suitcase are her outfits and a couple pairs of pajamas. Please hang them up as soon as possible so they don't get wrinkled. I must go now. Benji's waiting."

Her favorite toy, knowing how ridiculous the thought of Courtney knowing what her new dog's favorite toy was when she didn't even know her own husband's favorite color.

"Oh," she remembered, "one more thing." Reaching outside, pulling in a what looked like a small four poster doggy bed, she laid it on the floor beside the other items.

Tiptoeing backward toward the front door as if not to upset Peanut who looked on, comfortably clutched in the safety of Tora's hold. "Call my cell if you need me," she whispered. Blowing an air kiss, she disappeared behind the closing front door.

"When will you be back?" Tora asked the empty hall in self-amusement.

Holding this little pup out at arm's length, Tora examined her cuteness as Peanut seemed to do the same to her. Her tiny black nose and thin shiny black lips, which looked to be smiling, and those innocent little brown eyes staring back melted Tora's heart.

Smitten, she could not be mad at her selfish sister. This charming little pup had no idea what was in store for it with Courtney.

"Don't you worry little girl. I'll take good care of you while your mommy's gone." Pulling Peanut close to her, she gave her a tiny hug in fear of hurting this fragile creature.

She'd never had a puppy, nor had she ever held any living creature this small. Feeling attached already, Tora was familiar with being pushed off on someone else by Courtney.

As children, it was Courtney's responsibility to look after her little sister when playing outside. Tora was often pawned off to the senile neighbor down the block, Mrs. Gladstone. Tora found it odd when every few minutes the woman looked confused to see her there, sitting quietly at her small, round kitchen table. Repeatedly the kind woman would offer her cookies from a box with a picture of a Jack Russell Terrier on it.

Tora knew one thing for sure, she did not like the taste of those cookies.

"It's you and me now kid," she said, giving Peanut another gentle squeeze before gently placing her down on the floor. "Let's go make a cup of tea."

Scurrying across the tile floor to keep up with Tora, Peanut happily followed her into the kitchen. Grabbing a mug from the cabinet, Tora turned to find Peanut in a full squat, peeing on her crème colored tiled floor. Something about a dog in pearls, a sweater and tiara relieving herself made Tora laugh out loud.

Calmly laying down the mug, she grabbed the paper towels from the counter. "Housebroken," she sighed, repeating her sister's words and shaking her head. Tora couldn't help but laugh when thinking to herself how everyone in her life seemed so selfish lately.

Chapter

9

It had been a long first day with the students return to the classroom. Courtney had added an extra week to her trip which left Peanut in Tora's care longer than planned.

Although it had gotten better, it was a messy first few days for Tora. She was welcomed back home daily by her energetic house guest who was always bearing *gifts*; small puddles of pee and pebbles of poop were often sprinkled throughout her home. Looking on the brighter side, at least it wasn't on carpet and thankfully Peanut wasn't a Great Dane. How funny would it be to name your Great Dane *Peanut*?

Upon returning home, Tora would be met by a very happy, unclothed Peanut at her feet. Today was no different.

Lifting Peanut up with a swoop of her hand, she gave her a little peck on the head. "If Courtney saw you now, she would say you were naked," Tora chuckled.

The sight of Peanut without an outfit on did seem a bit strange, considering how she was dressed when they first met. Her lack of clothing also made her look more fragile.

Cradling Peanut, she slowly crept around the house, checking the floors for *gifts*.

To Tora's delight, the floors were clean.

"Good job!" she praised a tail wagging Peanut.

Grabbing her pink leash from the Doggy Haven bag, Tora clipped it onto Peanut's diamond collar, and they went for a walk.

Tora read the best way to get Peanut to keep her business outside would be to let her smell what the other dogs in the neighborhood were doing. A perfect spot was right across the street from her home and she had been taking Peanut there every morning, after work and then one last time before settling in for the night. It served a purpose for the other dogs in the neighborhood, so why not Peanut?

Together they jogged across the street as fast as Peanut's little legs would allow.

Peanut sniffed and paced the area, picking up each strange, new scent. Letting her go in her own yard crossed Tora's mind, but she knew how urine could ruin the grass. She decided it was best to save that convenience for rainy nights or when she was just too tired. It was only for a week or two at the most she imagined, and she needed the exercise anyway.

"That dog is adorable!" A woman's voice squealed out in delight.

Tensing up her shoulders, Tora slowly turned towards the loud voice. *Could it be?* She found herself face to face with none other than Rebecca.

"Thank you?" Tora replied, as she gave a quick look around to make sure it was indeed her this woman was speaking to.

"You live across the street, yes?" Rebecca asked, cocking her brow.

Tora knew this anomaly from her neighborhood performances of pounding the pavement almost every day, but Rebecca knew *her?* How? Why?

Taken aback, and a bit flattered, she paused before answering, "Yes. Yes, I do."

"I've seen you and your husband. I never saw this cutie though," she said, kneeling down and giving Peanut a pet after finishing up her business. "I'm Jill." She enthusiastically introduced herself.

So that was her name.

"Tora," she smiled, now introducing herself.

"Tora," Jill repeated, looking away for a moment in thought. "I've never heard that name before," she said, looking back at Tora, bobbing her head in approval. "I like it!"

Jill seemed happy. A little much for Tora, but her wish came true. Here she was chatting it up with her neighbor. "It's actually Victoria," Tora corrected. "My mother used to call me Tora for short. It stuck."

"It's different," Jill said, rising to her feet. "Different is good. So, you and your hubby got a new pooch? I love her diamond collar. It makes her look classy, regal. She looks like a celebrity dog."

Jill, who already seemed to be hyper and full of energy, probably from her neighborhood power walks, now confirmed this in her spunky talk.

Tora knew if Courtney could have heard her little Peanut referred to as a Celebrity Dog, and from this *Celebrity Neighbor* of all people, well, she would be tickled her favorite color. As far as the hubby went, Tora felt conflicted about telling her the truth; the whole truth anyway.

Oh, screw it. Not that she owed this woman any explanations, but why lie? If the truth ever were to come out Tora knew she would look like a fool. She had enough of that for a lifetime now. "Peanut is actually my sister's dog. I'm dog sitting," she humbly admitted, avoiding any husband talk hoping Jill didn't push it any further.

"Peanut!" Jill shrieked. "Oh My God! That is just so darn cute and very fitting for this petite cutie pie. She is a real girl's dog. How does your husband like her?"

Not only was Jill friendly, she was nosey. Other than being inquisitive, Jill seemed observant. Had she not seen Dane's car absent from the driveway these past two months? He could have been dead for all she knew. Maybe that was what prompted her to ask.

"He hasn't seen the dog. We broke up."

Jill cocked her head back.

"Me and my husband too!" she exclaimed. "What a coincidence. Well, I don't know whether to say I'm sorry or congratulations," she cackled, "but if you ever want to vent, husband bash or just talk about it, I pass your house everyday honey. Give me a shout. I could always use a break."

That floored Tora. Jill and her husband broke up? It had to be Jill, who did the dumping. She couldn't understand what man in their right mind would leave Jill, who was clearly a trophy wife, or at least that's how she saw it. Maybe it was the voice. Tora could see that becoming irritating over time.

It became apparent to Tora after Dane cheated, the true values in a wife weren't what mattered. Men seemed to have this delusion about themselves, as if they were some sort of prize. More like a booby prize.

Her own father, who was a pretty good husband before her parents separated, considered himself a rolling stone, just like the song, and after a while took off to find himself. Tora hadn't seen that rolling stone in years, and then she had heard through the grapevine that he'd passed away. She still had her mother, though, who preferred to be called Marie.

For some reason her mother, Marie, took offense to being referred to as someone's mother. While it didn't bother Tora as a child, it seemed unthinkable to her now that she was an adult.

Tora, who longed to have children, wanted so terribly to be called Mom, or Ma, any label that associated her with being a mother. Yet her own mother didn't feel the same.

Marie also didn't seem to care when the rolling stone of a husband grabbed his hat and rolled on out. She never seemed happy with him anyway and they were both so different. There are some things you don't pick up on when you are a child. Your parents are just your parents. You never wonder if they are happy, because as a child, *your* happiness is all that matters.

So, while Tora learned most men were never satisfied, she also discovered most women seemed to be okay staying the course with the balding, potbellied older versions of the stud they thought they married. Some women were even struggling at home with men that didn't want to work.

Why was it that women could settle for less when they were the ones who usually deserved more?

Maybe her parents weren't so odd after all. Maybe Tora just needed therapy. Then she realized Rebecca, or rather *Jill*, could be her support group.

They could be each other's support. How close and convenient would this be. Tora was thrilled and she saw such promise.

Jill could help Tora get through her separation and Tora could do the same for Jill, while subtly working on changing Jill's voice. Baby steps.

"I'd like that," Tora smiled modestly, while inside she was ecstatic to join forces with a woman who could finally have some compassion toward what she was going through.

"My next stroll I'll drop my number in your mailbox. Shoot me a text when you get it and then I'll have your number too," she beamed, raising her sculpted shoulders in delight.

Jill seemed easy to talk to. Just meeting her today made Tora feel as if she'd known her for years. It felt so natural, but Jill did seem like a lot. Her exuberance alone was that of a toddler, and Tora already felt drained from what could not have been more than five minutes of conversing.

Then again, this was exactly what she wanted. What she had been planning as she watched this perfect woman pass her house just about every day. Why not at least try it? Maybe all Tora needed was someone in her life with some zest, and boy, did Jill have plenty of that.

"OK," nodding to her new friend. "Sounds like a plan."

"Bye Peanut!" Jill said, giving a little wave, then blowing a kiss which reminded Tora of her sister Courtney, especially when Jill walked backwards and turned robotically picking back up her speed walking.

"So that was the infamous Rebecca," Tora said to herself, thinking about their encounter. Walking back into her house, she unhooked Peanut who then bolted for the living room. Peanut hopped up on the black leather sofa waiting for Tora to join her. They already had a routine.

"She isn't with her husband either Peanut." Tora said aloud as she prepared her tea.

Tora had thought she saw Jill's husband once or twice in his car and an occasional couple's power walk around the block. He was a looker himself. A trophy husband if there was such a thing. A Ken to Jill's Barbie.

She was interested to learn what broke those two up, and in time she would find out.

Completing her tea with a splash of milk, Tora grabbed her tote bag from the dining room chair and headed over to the sofa to sit with Peanut. Rummaging through her cluttered bag for her cell phone, Tora felt the need to text Donna. She wanted to let her know who she'd just run into.

This was a good way to reestablish some type of communication with her friends, who had kept a bit of distance since the breakup. Tora only wanted her friendships back to normal as well as her life. She figured this would be a good start.

Pulling up Donna's contact on her phone, she stared at the picture that popped up on the screen. Sarcastic and purse lipped, a look she was known for, made Tora think again.

While the women were always joking and mocking the very fit, attractive Jill, there probably wasn't much of a chance the women would be as thrilled to meet her as Tora was. That wouldn't be very fair or smart, throwing Jill to the wolves so soon.

Maybe she wouldn't share this information after all. Not yet anyway.

Chapter

10

Sitting on the floor of her living room surrounded by old photos, Tora could have easily been mistaken for an overflowing hamper.

Trying on clothes earlier in the day, here she sat wearing layers on top of layers of clothing from her closet of mishaps. With her too short yoga pants, colorful socks, ill-fitting tops, and a beanie under a floppy hat, she looked ridiculous. Finally finding a use for that vibrant skirt, she had it draped around her neck as a scarf.

When the doorbell rang, Tora's head bobbed up as if she had just got caught with her hand in the cookie jar. Knowing she was a sorry sight, she quickly tried to collect the scattered photos and albums and toss them back in their box, but she was only making more of a mess.

As the doorbell chimed again, Peanut took notice this time, running and slipping along the slippery ceramic tiled floor toward the door. She was barking ferociously, or as ferociously as a Yorkie could bark.

"Shit!" Tora exclaimed, quickly shoving it all to the side. What if it was Dane? She did not want to be seen like this.

Bogged down with layers upon layers of clothing, Tora struggled to get up, then practically limped her way to the door. Seeing a slim woman's image through the glass she slowly opened it. Peanut stopped barking.

"Hi!" Jill beamed, wearing her signature black workout ensemble, "Nice hat," she complimented, standing there perfectly coiffed, flashing those pearly whites of hers.

Dazed and slightly out of breath, Tora pulled off the floppy hat, then the knit beanie. A few strands of Tora's hair stood on end from the static electricity, but Jill ignored it. Tossing them both behind the door, she was trying to keep her composure, totally forgetting about the many other items she was wearing.

"Want to walk?" Jill asked, continuing to walk in place to keep those calories burning overlooking the fact that Tora looked like a walking clothes rack.

Down in the dumps, Tora lacked the energy and the desire to join the ever-effervescing Jill. She seemed like a lot of work on a regular day, today would be almost impossible.

"Hmm. I'm just not up to it today."

"OK," Jill shrugged, poking her head in a bit to see if anyone else was inside.

"Want to come in?" The words came out before Tora's brain could think.

"Sure," she chirped and walked right in.

"Organizing?" she asked, slowly approaching the pile of photos strewn across the floor.

Tora rolled her eyes, feeling embarrassed and self-loathing. "More like reminiscing."

Curious, Jill bent over what looked like photo album vomit. Her eyes scanned over the many pictures. Most of the photos were of Tora and Dane; holidays, vacations, or one of the many nights out with their friends.

Closing the door, "Maybe I should just throw them all away." Tora said under her breath.

Jill appeared concentrated on one photo. It was of Tora and Dane just waking up in what looked like a hotel room, still in pajamas and messy hair. Suddenly Jill tossed it to the side as if she no longer had use for it herself.

"Should I?" she asked again.

Jill looked at Tora. "Should you what?"

"The pictures. Should I throw them away?"

"No," she scolded, looking up at her. "This is your life. These are pictures of you. When you're eighty, you will want to look back. See who you were with, where you were. Your youth. Your beauty."

Beauty? Did Jill think she was beautiful? She hadn't heard that from anyone in a long time. It made her feel good, as a matter of fact, it made her feel great, especially coming from someone as attractive as Jill.

Jill was right. In her senior years, Tora would look back and think about these pictures and this moment with Jill. She would regret having let sadness and disappointment affect all she had going for her right now. She couldn't let that happen. Her future self wouldn't allow it.

Jill was wise. Tora needed to hang around more with this woman who represented hope in an otherwise hopeless situation. Giving off a good vibe, Tora was drawn to her new friend's positive energy. If it only came in lower doses.

"This one is nice." she said, holding one of Tora with "The Three Amigas" and their husbands at Ali's annual Christmas tree trimming party. Leaning in to get a better look, Tora wondered herself, who had taken that picture since they were all in it, but she couldn't remember.

Tora felt warm and fuzzy seeing that photo. It was from a better time in her life. She and the other women were smiling. They all looked so happy. The men held up their beers in inebriated celebration. Even Jill appeared to feel the merriment, the happiness of friendship the photo conveyed as she looked it over. A little envy maybe?

What was Tora going to do now on holidays, birthdays, vacations? Thanksgiving would be the next occasion since the split. It was still early, but Tora hadn't heard a word from Donna, who hosted it every year.

Was Tora going to get invited? Would she go? Dane may be there, and with his new girlfriend no doubt. Maybe he would be off some place doing whatever her tradition was. Probably skiing in Aspen, or something snobby like that. Either way, it would be strange.

"Men," Jill sighed with a tinge of disgust in her voice. Releasing the photo from her fingers, it drifted back down onto the pile.

"Let's shop," she suddenly blurted out, spinning around. A reckless look filled her eyes.

"OK," Tora agreed. She could handle Jill's sunny disposition and hyper personality, at least for a little while. Maybe it would wear off on her.

"Can I use your bathroom?" Jill asked, crossing her legs like a child unable to hold it in. "I drink a lot of water and once I stop moving …" she said, bobbing her head from shoulder to shoulder.

"Sure, down the hall to your right."

"Thanks!" She smiled and flew down the hall.

Neatly, Tora collected the last of the pictures and closed the lid of the box. Her sorrow temporarily washed away.

"Do you have dandruff?" Jill asked loudly, rejoining Tora back in the living room while clutching a large bottle of dandruff shampoo. "Because I know a good remedy."

"No, that's my husband's," Tora sheepishly admitted.

Jill looked at Tora blankly for a moment. "Your ex's stuff is still here? Why?"

"He hasn't picked it up yet."

Her face had a pained and puzzled look, "Why is this stuff still here?" she asked, shaking the bottle with conviction.

"He hasn't picked it up yet. His clothes are still here too," she said, watching Jill's eyes bulge with fury and frustration.

"This is not a storage container. Do you have a box? Or better yet, a garbage bag?"

Tora knew exactly what Jill was getting at. Heading for the kitchen, Tora slid out a large black garbage bag from under the sink. Together they headed to the bathroom, tossing all of Dane's personal items inside.

Next they walked to the bedroom and Tora opened the top drawer of the dresser before looking at Jill. They dug their hands in pulling out anything and everything that looked like it belonged to a man and right into the bag it went.

"I can't throw these out," Tora grimaced. The thought of throwing her cheating husband's stuff out somehow seemed wrong.

Jill turned to Tora and smiled sinisterly. "We're not throwing it out. We're delivering it. And the embarrassing stuff? That goes right on top."

Jill was as premeditated as she was vicious. Not only did it feel good cleansing her home of anything Dane owned, it was liberating to take back all this space taken up by Dane who hadn't been home for weeks. All these memories left behind to remind her of him, every minute of every day, as if he left items there on purpose.

"Maybe he's too lazy to pick this crap up, or it makes him feel like he still belongs. Either way, it's got to go," she ordered, as they moved onto the next draw dumping all male related items into the large garbage bag like the garbage it was.

"Why should you have to look at this stuff? You are being constantly reminded of him. Do you think there are any reminders of you where he is? Not only is it unfair to you, he is also keeping his territory marked. Like a cat that pisses all over!" It appeared Jill had some unresolved issues herself.

Tora hadn't looked at it that way before. She knew everything Jill was saying was right, and while Tora had reservations about carelessly tossing Dane's belongings in a bag, he hadn't been coming for them. How important could they be? He must have had new dandruff shampoo wherever he was staying. Heck, he probably had a whole new wardrobe and was never coming back for any of his stuff; just like he was never coming back for her.

Jill stopped for a moment and looked at Tora. "Is there a chance you guys will get back together?"

"No," Tora replied without hesitation.

"So, let's do this shit!" she cheered.

Riled up now, Tora went back to the kitchen for more black bags. Upon returning, she found Jill sitting on the floor, looking at a photo she was holding in her hand. "Who's this?" she asked, holding the photo out to Tora.

Taking the picture, Tora looked at the photo of a young boy, maybe six or seven, with a head of brown curly hair and light blue eyes. Not recognizing the boy in the old photo, she turned it over to read the name Scotty, written in pen.

"Where did you find this?"

"In this box."

In Jill's other hand was a beaten-up shoe box. Tora had never seen that before either. Inside was an old pocketknife, a few rusted fishhooks, a small box of stick matches, and a couple of movie stubs, all of which told her it was old, but sentimental junk.

"It was in the last drawer under that fleece blanket," Jill said, tilting her head toward the open drawer with the blanket hanging out.

Tora remembered that faded blue fleece blanket. Dane had referred to it as his "lucky blanket". He had used it for those cold night fishing trips with the boys, but she never checked to see if anything was hiding underneath. Why should she? And while she appreciated Jill's help, why was she opening closed boxes. That was an invasion of privacy, but then again, so was going through his drawers.

Tora then wondered if she had allowed her husband too much privacy. She also couldn't help but wonder if this was this one of those Aha moments? She didn't even want to think of the chance that, or the possibility of -

"I'm not sure who this is," she said, handing the photo back to Jill as if she didn't have her suspicions. "Put it back. Let's just pack it up with the rest." Walking to the mirrored closet, she opened the side where Dane's clothing hung.

Placing the photo back inside the box, Jill closed the lid and rested it on the pile of clothing inside the bag. Yanking the blanket roughly from the drawer, she rolled it up and shoved it in too.

"Leaving this stuff here just gives him a reason to come back and talk to you when his new shit falls apart, and it will. It will so fall apart," she said with a vengeance while rising to her feet.

While it felt so wrong, it felt so right. Angry and spiteful wasn't Tora, but why should she care what Dane thought about getting his old life back all crumpled up in a bag.

"My ex picks his stuff up. He has been at it for weeks. I just don't understand how he's not finished yet," Jill laughed as she continued to go through Dane's belongings like a pro, "but at least he's picking it up."

Tora sensed Dane was coming and going when she wasn't home just like Jill's husband. Little things here and there that she might not notice, only she did. She noticed his favorite baseball cap was missing from the coat hook in the mudroom. She noticed his collection of coins, which he hid in the pantry on the back shelf out of sight was also missing.

It was as if he thought Tora would cash its worthless contents in behind his back. Sneakily he took what he needed and then slithered out like the snake he was. Just as she was about to mention that to Jill, sure their next fiasco would be a trip to the hardware store, a half full garbage bag flew past her.

"Incoming!" Jill announced just as the bag plopped right at Tora's feet.

One by one, they filled each large, black garbage bag then dragged them to the front door.

"That was a workout in itself," Jill huffed. "Do you know where he is?"

"Probably work," Tora said, realizing this was really going to happen.

The plan was to drive to Dane's job, drop off everything he had in their home, right there in front of the office trailer.

Was it going to make her look bad? Angry? Possibly jealous or scorned?

She was all three at one time or another, Tora was getting used to what her husband did to her, so she didn't care. The hurt was slowly subsiding more and more each day. Getting rid of these reminders might help the healing process move along a little faster for Tora and be therapeutic for Jill too who seemed to get a thrill out of it.

"Ready?" Jill asked as she lugged one of the heavier black bags to the front door.

Tora was conflicted and it showed.

"Hey!" She reminded Tora, "He is lucky we aren't gathering all his embarrassing shit, and I know he must have some, and dropping that off at work for everyone to see; or worse yet, his girlfriend's house."

Tora could think of a few embarrassing items she could gather, such as Dane's hemorrhoid cream, which he used for the puffiness under his eyes. No one would have known that, and if they did, that may have been even more embarrassing for a man than using it for actual hemorrhoids.

He also had a few pairs of novelty underwear tucked away, like his superhero boxers, which had a little cape attached to the back. Then there were the items Tora knew Dane was super sensitive about, such as his denture case that held his partial plate after a teenage hockey accident knocked out a few of his teeth from the eye tooth back, and an expired box of Efferdent. Pretty sure that was a big sore spot for Dane, so yeah, Jill was right, Dane was getting off easy.

Nodding to each other the two headed outside to the car. Tossing the four large, heavy garbage bags into Tora's trunk, they headed to the drop.

Jill gave Tora the confidence and reassurance she needed to feel strong, and to take a stand regarding the damage Dane caused. These past months he had gotten away clean. Dane had the freedom to live his new life without being harassed or interrupted by Tora, who had been a prisoner in her own head. Now it was time to rock his world a little.

Searching for tunes on the radio, the energy in the car was on high. They were both fresh out of their marriages and they both felt as if they had scores to settle. Jill turned up the radio, and the ladies began to sing.

"You're no good, you're no good, you're no good, baby your no good," they sang, belting out tunes the whole ride there.

Pulling up to the trailer, Jill lowered the radio and instructed, "Pop the trunk."

Pressing the small button below her steering wheel, Tora felt like she had just pulled the tab on a hand grenade.

Hearing the click, Jill jumped out of the car and disappeared in the back.

Tora sat in her seat with the car running. Silently she prayed Dane wouldn't come out.

Jill lugged each bag to the bottom of the trailer's roll-away, metal stairway.

Tora still wondered if she was doing the right thing. It triggered a memory of the day her sister Courtney told her how fun it would be to pour the whole bottle of Mister Bubble into the running bath water.

Paralyzed with fear, Tora could only watch as the foam elegantly bubbled over the sides of the tub and onto the floor slowly covering the tips of her toes.

Courtney, like the drama queen she was, ran frantically to summon their mother excited to share with her what baby Tora had done.

Tora could still remember her mother's panic, seeing her small daughter now almost waist deep in bubbles. Pushing her way through the slippery suds, her mother leaned in and disappeared into the swell of overflow. She had to feel around blindly for the knobs to shut off the water.

That incident resulted in no dessert for a week and nightmares. Courtney told frightening stories about why their mother was sick all the time and peeing bubbles because of swallowing them and how it was all Tora's fault.

The car rocked, followed by a slam and Jill hopped back into the car. Turning to Tora, she gave one nod and a sly grin, "Done."

"Cheers!" they said in unison as their coffee mugs clinked together. They sat at the outdoor coffee shop feeling proud of themselves. They had successfully completed their mission.

"I should have removed at least nine articles of clothing before we left the house." Tora said, slipping the colorful skirt off from around her shoulders.

"Eight now, but who's counting." Jill joked. "I got lucky you weren't out with your friends today. I haven't seen them as much as I used to either. What's up with that?" she asked, sipping her coffee.

Starting from the beginning, Tora told Jill how she and Dane had met. How she'd been instantly drawn to Dane, whose real name was Daniel, but called himself Dane because of his love for the beauty of the Great Dane dog breed.

She continued, going into detail about how Dane and their friends all knew each other from childhood, and how they formed what she only could describe as a family.

She then shared stories of feeling like a leper at times, and Dane's workaholic behavior that led to the encounter she had with Sam that hit her like a pie in the face.

Her cheeks reddened. Tora could feel her body temperature rising, causing her upper lip to bead up with sweat. Tora spoke about leaving her husband's hospital room with her tail between her legs after feeling less than the woman that stood before her, and then a coward afterward.

Finally, Tora explained how being a teacher made her disappear for a while every year. How it was difficult to see her friends anyway, but as she heard herself say it, she realized it sounded like she was making excuses for their absences, and she was.

"If you ever needed friends, it would be now."

Jill was right again. Donna, Ali, and especially Kate, should have made more of an effort to see her and check on her after all that had happened. In the past, they would show up at her door unexpectedly. Now she was lucky if she was getting a text every few days.

"Thanks for today." Tora said, lifting her mug up to Jill. "To you." She said, clinking mugs with Jill once more.

Jill smiled and before taking a sip said, "No. This one is for you."

Chapter

11

"I wish you would have told me what you were going to do before you did it!" Donna squawked into the cell phone.

Quickly pulling her cell phone from her ear, Tora smiled as she waved goodbye to Jill, who walked home from Tora's instead of being driven to burn more calories. Slowly raising her phone back to her ear, her face soured hearing her friend's grating voice.

"What did I do, Donna?" Closing the door behind her, Tora knelt to lift Peanut who pawed at her legs like a toddler begging their mother to pick them up.

"You embarrassed him at work Tor. How could you put his stuff in garbage bags like that?

"I embarrassed him?" Tora shrieked. "I embarrassed him?" Finding Donna's reason for concern laughable, "Think about what you are saying here, Donna." Proceeding to make her tea.

"Was that necessary?" Speaking to Tor as though she were a child.

"I suppose he wanted them neatly folded in suitcases." Tora retorted. Did anyone reprimand Dane? Pretty self-assured and on a Jill high, Tora would not be taking any bull from Donna today.

"I don't know Tora. Why couldn't you just leave it there? After all, he is still paying the bills."

Her jaw clenched, "How do you know that?"

Donna had made a good point though. Dane was paying the bills as well as the mortgage. Maybe she should have left his stuff alone.

No! No! No! He should have picked up his stuff a long time ago. This the least that liar could do! Don't let her brainwash you!

"You made yourself look bad, that's all I'm saying."

Tora balled up her fists and squeezed until she felt the burn of her fingernails almost breaking the skin.

"So, let me get this straight. Dane cheating on me made him look good. Allowing him to leave his shit here, uh, that didn't that make me look bad? Like I'm just sitting here waiting for him to come back. But dropping his stuff off, that made me look bad?"

Donna was silent.

"Why are you calling me, anyway? Did Dane tell you to call me?"

"This isn't like you. What has gotten into you?" Donna questioned, ignoring Tora's comments.

"He cheated on me Donna. For months, maybe even years. Maybe the entire marriage. He got away with MURDER! Maybe I'm just tired of being lied to." Her voice cracked.

Don't cry Tora! Hold in those tears! Anything you do or say in a moment of weakness will get right back to Dane. Donna is the enemy right now. Be tough girl, you got this!

"And you took that Rebeca with you!" Donna hissed like a tire with a slow leak.

How did Donna know that? Did Dane see them? Did Donna follow them?

"I wouldn't trust that woman Tor," Donna continued.

Tora had just as much loyalty to a new friend as Donna had to an old one. "Her name is Jill, and you haven't even met her. And that's another thing, you guys are just so engrossed in your own little world that you don't leave room for anyone else! You're all so, so, … clannish!"

Tora spoke from the heart. It was hard to forget the miserable look on Donna's face that night six years ago when Dane introduced her to his friends. Kate and Ali, who weren't very welcoming themselves, were just following Donna's lead. Donna was a boss; a bully. If she didn't like you, neither did the other two. Now, Tora's fate in the group was in the hands of Donna once more.

"Just take care of yourself Tora."

There it was again! *Just take care of yourself Tora.* Ali told her that very same thing in the park.

Feeling the vibration of her cell phone, she quickly checked her caller ID. It was Courtney. This was the call she was dreading.

"Courtney's calling me Donna. I have to go."

Ending her call with Donna and switching over to her sister was something Tora would never have done in the past. The thought of Donna throwing her cell phone on the floor and stomping all over it flashed through her mind, but she didn't care. She even found it funny. Not only had Tora heard enough, but as a member of this small, elite group, Tora knew her membership was about to expire. A membership she had no interest in renewing.

"What's up, Court?"

"I'm home! I cannot wait to see my little angel," she sang out, sounding happy for a change. "How is she doing?"

Silently mimicking her sister, Tora was not pleased to hear how eager Courtney sounded. Secretly Tora had hoped Courtney would just forget about her, just like she did with her turtle, the saltwater fish, and the parakeet Courtney agreed to watch for one of Ben's cousins away on vacation. Leaving the window open, that little birdie flew out and was never seen again. Which posed the question, *why was Courtney looking for Peanut?*

"She is doing well." Giving Peanut a snuggle while trying to hide her disappointment.

"I have the vet on the way over. I totally forgot I made this well check-up. You get them for free when you adopt from New Yorkie. Get it? We drove to New York to get her. Do you think you could bring her over? I'm exhausted from the trip. Pretty please?"

Here we go again, more requests from the Courtney Favors Castle. Would it be too much to ask Courtney to pick up her own dog? Her sister was exhausted from having too much fun, but Tora was exhausted herself, from actual work and the shit show which was her life. And since when did Courtney care about free checkups?

"Ok. I'm coming," she said reluctantly.

Ending the call, Tora slid the phone in the back of her jeans pocket and rested Peanut on the floor. "I promise I will come and visit," she said, looking down at her tiny face.

Sadly, Tora collected Peanut's things and placed them into her little suitcase as Peanut sat and watched. Grabbing her own tote bag, she scooped Peanut up in her hand and headed out the door. Tossing the bags in her trunk, Tora secured Peanut in her special doggy car seat and they set off to Courtney's.

Every few minutes Tora would look back at her precious cargo, making sure Peanut was still safely buckled up behind her. With her little pink travel bag beside her, clueless as to where she was going, Tora wondered if Peanut would miss her too.

Chapter

12

Tora was thankful she had Jill to meet with almost every day after work. Not only was it fun, it was also distracting. It kept her from over thinking, especially now that Peanut was gone, leaving Tora and her thoughts home together by themselves.

"Just weeks ago, you were huffing and puffing just from speed walking. Now you're jogging and barely breaking a sweat." Jill proudly reminded Tora, as they jogged the neighborhood together, side by side.

A large white sedan slowly rolled up alongside of the women, "Who's your friend Jill?" a rather stocky fellow called out from the open driver's side window.

"I'm telling your girlfriend!" Jill flirtatiously warned, wagging her finger at him.

"Which one?" he laughed before speeding off.

Tora could tell Jill relished the attention. Attention she must have got every day Tora would guess.

Turning to Tora, "I have to pee." Jill suddenly announced. "Do you mind if we stop at my house? I drank a lot of water today. I don't know if I can hold it."

"No, not at all. Go pee."

Jogging until they reached the front of Jill's home, a cute one family home that looked much like her own. The front had a few small bushes under the windows and an evenly dispersed array of mums bordered along the short walkway leading to her gray bricked stoop. "I'll be right out."

Tora looked on as a swipe of Jill's hand unlocked her front door in a cool and fancy way, then she disappeared inside.

Putting this time to good use, Tora used the front step to stretch out her calves. She'd been feeling better than she had for a long time. Now, exercising regularly, having healthy lunches, going for coffee and shopping, along with a whole new wardrobe, one that fit her shrinking waistline, it was as if her life had finally found its new normal.

The sound of tires rolling along Jill's driveway caught Tora's attention. Turning, she watched as a black Mazda pulled in. Stepping out was a dapper suit wearing business type.

Shutting the car door, he slid his keys in his pants pocket with a cool slickness. "Can I help you?" he asked, walking toward Tora.

"Oh, I'm waiting for a friend," she innocently replied, wondering why he asked, followed by wondering why she answered.

A questionable look came across the man's sturdy face. "You're waiting for Jill?" he asked, as if he wanted her to repeat it again, just to be sure. "Don't you live around the block, over on Harley?"

Assuming the man had recognized her from the neighborhood, "Yes, and yes," she answered.

"Shut up, Tora! Stop answering his questions! He could be a serial killer! A well-dressed one at that!"

Suddenly Jill appeared, "I'm ready," she announced, briskly running down the steps, passing right by the well-dressed man standing outside of her home as if he were invisible. "Let's go," she ordered Tora, sticking her nose up in the air, shimmying her tiny waist down the street.

Tora had no idea what to make of this odd encounter, but if Jill was ignoring him, maybe she should too. She followed her friend down the block.

"You two are hanging out together?" his raised voice echoed in the distance.

Walking faster, it was as if Jill didn't want to be in earshot of anything he might say.

"Who was that?" Tora asked, keeping up with Jill's quick steady pace. "Was that, is he, *your husband?*"

"Yes. That's Marc," she snapped between breaths. "Coming to pick up more of his stuff, I suppose. I don't even want to see his freakin' face. I walk every day around this time to get out of the house so he can come and go smoothly. I see today he was a little earlier than usual."

"He was dressed really nice. What does he do?" Tora asked curiously.

"He works at a bank. He secures mortgages and stuff like that. He makes pretty good money to buy his Italian suits, and his shoes, and eat at fancy schmancy restaurants."

Jill was visibly annoyed. Tora still hadn't learned why her new friend and her husband were no longer together. All of that walking and talking always seemed to focus on Tora and her troubles. Jill had a story as well, but didn't everyone?

She had wanted to ask about their split when they first started their walks, but the intensity always made it difficult to hold a conversation. Huffs, puffs and sniffles was all Tora could manage in the beginning.

Now, Tora could walk and talk. She just didn't have the nerve to ask her friend what happened with her marriage, so instead she thought of the photo Jill found in a shoe box she'd never seen. Plenty of people had a junk drawer or a box they tossed things into, but Tora felt there was some secrecy about it.

Her thoughts then changed to Peanut. She missed her terribly. Once again, she thought about visiting the local shelters. She thought about what she would eat for dinner, and if she should buy a new pair of running shoes.

They walked a good thirty minutes in silence before Jill led them down blocks that would take them back to their homes and straight up Tora's walkway.

"Whew! I feel great!" Jill exclaimed, now seeming to change back to her old self.

Putting her hands on her waist, Tora bent over in exhaustion. "I hope I don't drop dead when I go inside." kicking out her legs to cool off.

"It's not good to suddenly stop walking, especially after that brisk pace we kept. The good thing is we torched a lot of calories just now. I will keep moving and head home, don't forget to drink water."

Giving Jill a thumbs up, Tora's tired legs barely made it up the three steps.

"If you aren't doing anything later, text me. We can have some wine and unwind. We deserve it!"

With a smile on her lips, walking backwards and making silly googly eyes, Jill let out a loud cackle. Spinning around like she usually did when excited, Jill sped off like she had to pee again and galloped off towards home.

Painfully making it inside, Tora headed straight to the fridge. Opening a bottle of water, she put it to her lips and chugged it down.

A hot soak in the tub bath to help relax her achy muscles followed by wine at Jill's was her plan. It would be the perfect opportunity to ask what her husband meant by his remark.

Chapter 13

"Lovely," Tora acknowledged, as she entered her new friend's home for the first time.

Although the layout of their homes was the same, Jill's design and furnishings gave it an eclectic feel. It had no theme, no blended color scheme, yet it still flowed. It reminded Tora of something one might see on the set of a television show, or in a magazine. It most definitely suited Jill.

A large white faux fur rug lay perfectly atop the lackluster parquet flooring beneath an old apothecary coffee table in the center of the living room. There were large, bulky pillows in fun colors arranged along a crisp white sofa. On the other side was a rose petal patterned sitting chair. A few purple and red throw blankets draped here and there. An array of pictures hung from the walls, secured in mismatched frames.

What Tora noticed most were the books. They were everywhere. There were books on shelves, books on the coffee table, one was even sitting on the chair. Some were standing lined up in a row, others lay on their sides. Books that seemed to be placed for decor rather than for reading or having been read.

Subdued lighting came from a large stained-glass Tiffany style standing lamp set off in the far corner. The dim yellow light it emitted made it seem later than it was, much like the lighting of Tora's grandmother's home. Only this was Jill's home and she was no grandmother.

"I like the feel." Tora said, sinking into the deep sofa. "You have a nice vibe going on in here. It's comfy," she added, wanting to pull over one of the throw blankets and take a nap.

Jill smiled, handing Tora a glass of red wine. "Thanks Tora, that really means a lot," she answered, joining her at the opposite end of the sofa.

Tora raised her glass. "I see you live on the edge."

"Eh, it's just furniture." Jill shrugged, lifting her own glass. "It's nice to know you feel the ambience we tried to create. Marc and I always wanted a home where people could walk in for the first time and feel comfortable. We have been in many homes that felt cold, and I don't mean the temperature. What you are saying tells me we succeeded."

Tora couldn't help but pick up a hint of regret in her friend's softened voice.

"When I was growing up, I couldn't touch anything. I used to wonder why my parents bought furniture we couldn't sit on," Jill laughed. "Nothing matched, much like this place," waving her arm around in front of her. "Then I learned nothing matched because everything was given to us. Different people with different tastes. We couldn't sit on the furniture because what we had was meant to last. Now, I can buy my own. I like furniture that reminds me of my family. We weren't rich. We weren't even middle class. I just know we were safe. Safe and happy. This home became my safe happy space. It still is."

Rising from the sofa, Tora gravitated toward a red brick fireplace. She hadn't noticed it when she first walked in. It was small and stood tucked away in another corner of the room as if placed there temporarily. On its mantle were more books, and a few framed pictures of all different shapes, colors and sizes.

"I would sometimes see you guys together jogging." Tora mentioned as an afterthought, running her finger along the top of the flowery frame which held a picture of Jill and Marc, her arm in his. Dressed up as usual, she wore a black cocktail dress, he in a dark blue suit. Apart, they were attractive, but together they were on fire.

"Probably. We used to do a lot of things together." Jill buried her face in her wineglass. "Men. They seem to have their own little world going on inside those thick skulls of theirs. If we knew what was in there boy, we would probably run! Run far! Run fast!" She cackled into her glass.

"I was so blind." Tora said, still looking at the photo. "I put my husband on such a pedestal. Why didn't I demand the same back from him? I made him feel special." Tora told Jill, the only friend she felt she could say this too without being persecuted.

"Did he make you feel special?"

Turning, Tora smiled lazily. "He made me feel special, sometimes. Other times," she hesitated, inhaling the sweet aroma rising from her glass, "not so special. Actually, he made me feel horrible." Taking a quick sip to wash those words away.

Jill smirked, "As little girls we grow up thinking we will fall in love with this great guy, get married, have a gorgeous ring, a beautiful home, the most precious and smartest children in the world," letting out a snide laugh. "It's all bullschnit." Jill said, using her own version of the word, removing it's vulgarity. "Half the women I encounter say they wonder how they ended up with the jerk they did. Everyone and everything are a mess. Their health is poor. They gained too much weight. They are suffering, and everyone is just tired," shaking her head. "Wasted years," she sighed.

Tora knew about wasted years.

"Do you want him back?" Jill asked.

Tora had never asked herself that question before. She didn't really have an answer. Maybe she would have taken back the Dane she thought she'd had, but not the Dane she learned she had.

Wounded, "I just want my happy back." Tora frowned.

"Happiness is just an illusion sista. We are just as happy as we let ourselves be, and just as sad too."

Tora thought about Jill's words for a moment.

"I think that's all any of us want. Happiness," Jill sighed wistfully. "And while it sounds like such a simple request, happiness seems to be the hardest thing to acquire. Heck, I think I'd be able to win the lottery first," she laughed, shaking her head and sipping her wine.

At one time, Tora thought she was happy. Thinking about it now, it was as if her life was on pause. Spending time with people she had to, including her husband. It didn't seem to matter if she was there or not. Either way, it felt like work. Show up, smile, do your job, and go home.

Even Kate, who she considered a good friend, her best friend, could be standoffish when the others were around. It seemed as if they discussed how they would all treat her before she arrived. Tora was like that piece of the jigsaw puzzle you try to squeeze in. You know it doesn't fit but you force it any way.

Tora felt her own story was getting to sound like a broken record. How many times could she repeat it over and over before someone yelled, *ENOUGH!* What she wanted was to hear about Jill. With the help of her wine, she finally asked, "Why did you and Marc break up? I mean, if I'm not being too nosey. We always talk about me. We never talk about you."

Sinking back in her seat, Jill appeared to give that question careful thought.

"Well," Jill began, "Marc just started to get on my pucken nerves." She laughed loudly.

Jill's version of the F word amused Tora, who tried and failed to conceal her own loud laughter. She liked the way Jill played with words.

"We just started not getting along. I feel like he was picking up these bad habits or rather *annoying habits*."

"Like what?"

"Oh, you're really gonna make me go there," slurring her speech a little. "I hadn't given much thought to them lately. I find them extremely irritating and I am more than happy to forget about them, but since you asked, I will answer," she agreed, taking a breath and another sip of her wine as if to prepare for a long-winded reply.

"OK, this may sound trivial, but hear me out. Marc started leaving his stuff around for me to pick up. Socks, underwear, those little plastic flossy things," she said, scrunching up her face and clenching her teeth as if she had just been pinched. "That would get under my skin, but I'd ignore it. Then after a while, it was as if he just wanted to keep me busy. Like I didn't have enough to do. I have a health and fitness blog. It's become my job. I just don't leave the house for work or have set hours like he does. I could write for five hours or five minutes. I think he started to resent that. Or maybe he felt I wasn't really working since I was doing it from home. I would cook. Then he would leave his dishes on the table, the special seasonings he used, the newspaper he was reading. All of it. I was constantly cleaning up after him. I started to feel like his maid instead of his wife. It changes the relationship when you feel like the help. It changed my relationship that's for sure."

"I don't think that's trivial at all."

"Marriage has changed. Remember when only the men worked? Men made the rules. Well, some men think it's still like that. Stepping out of his pants, leaving them where they fell. Then he would complain to me if I left the blow dryer on the bathroom counter. Must I clean up after both you and me? Why don't you put the effin' blow dryer away?" she sneered.

The change in Jill's attitude also changed the pitch in her voice. Her anger seemed to build as her feelings came to the surface. It struck a nerve in Tora too, as her husband had done the same thing. If Tora left the paper sleeves to the tea bags on the counter, Dane wouldn't throw them away, he would just remind her she left them there.

"I loved, well, I still love my husband, but he made me feel invisible, useless, well other than cleaning up after him. I'd just had enough," Jill said, throwing up her free hand, "Eventually, we became more and more distant. Then, we started to bicker. In all honesty, I'd rather be alone. I like this," she said, folding her legs beneath her. "I have peace."

Smiling, Jill took a deep cleansing breath in. Exhaling, she looked around the room. "The place is always clean and neat now. If I want to eat, I eat. If I don't, I don't."

Jill made being separated sound good.

"So, you asked him to leave?"

Taking a sip of her wine, Jill shook her head no before swallowing. "It was a suggestion. A suggestion of his after we had a big fight one night. It was ridiculous too. Over a boot." She said, looking up at the ceiling as her eyes glistened. "It just got so petty after a while." She sniffled, blinking her eyes repeatedly before turning back to Tora. "You can be mad about a million important things and hold them all in, but it just takes that one little trigger," touching her forefinger to her thumb and holding it up in front of her, "to make the whole thing go poof," she said, separating her fingers and running her hand through the air like the finish to a magic act.

"A boot?"

"Once, in the middle of the night, I got up to pee. I walked down the hall to the bathroom and stubbed my toe on his snow boot. My pinky toe broke from the impact. There isn't much you can do about that right? Just tape it to your other toes."

Other than a fingernail, Tora had never broken anything.

"Yep." Jill held up her bare foot, admiring her wonky red nail polished pinky toe. "Nice and crooked now. Even after the tape."

"The broken toe was the last straw?"

"Well, it hurt like hell," she recalled. "I woke him up yelling and cursing and saying a lot of mean and nasty things." Shaking her shoulders as if she were shaking off a chill. "Looking back at it now, I shouldn't have said what I said. I was mad. I had just woken up, and that freaking' toe hurt!" She winced recalling the pain.

"But, I guess, that was the last straw for him, too." Jill shrugged, looking sad as she sipped her wine. "He packed a bag and left the next day."

Tora didn't know what to say. Jill looked like a lost little girl. A far cry from the energetic, confident woman she'd admired from her living room window every day.

"Plus, he was working a lot which made me feel like he didn't want to be home. Then when he was home, he was reading, or sleeping. Sometimes I would look at him sitting there," motioning toward the rose petal sitting chair across the room, wineglass in hand, swirling its contents around, "and I'd ask myself, who is that? Who the hell is that? It just wasn't a good energy in here. I don't respond well to that. Some women can do it, power through it, ya know? Not me," she said, shaking her head adamantly.

"I think those things are fixable. It all sounds like hurt feelings. The stress of being around each other too much. Everyone needs a break in between. Don't you think?'

While Jill's feelings were valid, Tora's husband cheated on her, and she just could not compare the two.

"Other than the toe, there was one more thing that Marc and I would argue over," she began, looking at Tora over her tipped glass as if she were hiding behind it. "He accused me of having an affair," and took a big gulp.

Now, Tora could compare. "He did?" her eyes bulged. "Were you?" she asked, walking back to the sofa she sat on the edge of her seat.

"Before I go on, I just want to tell you, I am so happy we met. I am ecstatic we became friends and can talk about this husband stuff."

"I am too Jill. You came into my life at a time when no one understood what I was going through. No one tried to either. It makes a difference when you and your husband break up and have the same friends. It's like who gets the dog?"

"Oh, I think I know who got the dog," her eyes narrowed. "Or should I say dogs," she laughed out loud. "Well, you have me now. I'm your friend Tora. You can tell me whatever you want, and I feel I can tell you whatever I want. What I need to tell you, and I really feel you will not judge me or jump to conclusions like my husband did."

"Of course! I never would." Tora assured her.

"And I want you to remember we are friends. Right Tora? You know we are friends, right?"

Those were Kate's words all over again, flooding her ears like pool water. It could have been the wine, but Tora started to feel there was more to Jill than meets the eye, and more to her story than she could ever imagine. But nothing Jill told Tora could make her look at her friend any differently. They were two peas in a pod; close to sisters. "Right," Tora firmly agreed.

"So, after a few months of bickering, going to bed mad, I met someone who -"

Interrupted by the ringing of Tora's cell phone, Jill stopped talking.

"Let me just see who it is."

Pulling out her cell phone from the back pocket of her jeans, Courtney's name appeared on the screen. If she didn't answer and there was no message, Tora would wonder all night if it were important. If she answered, it was likely Courtney needed a favor. Maybe she wanted to drop Peanut off. Now she had to answer it. "It's my sister. I'm sorry, it could be important."

Tora pushed herself up and out of the deep sofa seat, trying to balance her wine, her cell phone and herself. "Hey Court, what's up?" she asked into her phone, hoping for the best.

"Oh Tora, I had a big fight with Ben, can I come over?"

"I'm not home Court."

"You're not with those hideous friends of yours, are you? Don't tell them I had a fight with my husband. I don't want those idiots to know."

"I'm with Jill."

"Jill?"

"She lives around the corner from me …" Tora stated in a remindful tone.

"Oh, you're just around the corner from your house? Thank God! Meet me at your place. Ten minutes."

Tora didn't want to meet her sister. She wanted to stay at Jill's and hear all about whatever it was she was about to share. If two beautiful people like Jill and Marc had problems, well, anyone could have problems she figured.

"Please, Tora. I just need to talk to my sister." Courtney begged.

As selfish as Courtney was, Tora wasn't, especially when it came to her sister.

"OK Courtney." Tora sighed that familiar sigh.

"I'll bring coffee," she said, then hung up.

"Great." Tora said, clicking off the phone.

"Everything okay?"

"I have to go."

Jill slouched in her seat. "Oh, okay."

"What did you want to tell me?" Tora asked.

Jill looked up at Tora with her big brown eyes. "You know what, let's talk about it another time. It's a little long and there's a back story."

"Maybe we can pick up where we left off another night?" Tora asked, placing her glass down on the coffee table. "My sister needs me, and I feel like I was a little rude to her the other day."

"I often wish I had a sister. Then again, we could have been total opposites and hated each other. Sometimes the thought of something is much sweeter than the real thing. Like marriage. But yes, yes, I totally understand."

"Good night," she said, then let herself out. Jogging home, she figured she may as well burn off those unnecessary, empty calories.

The whole purpose of drinking wine was to relax, unwind, and get a little tipsy. Now she had to go home and listen to

Courtney do what she does best, talk about herself. She didn't need coffee for that. Just more wine.

Chapter

14

Tora awoke to an invigorating brisk fall morning and curled up snuggling with her new fluffy white comforter. She'd always wanted a white goose down comforter; too expensive for her being so frugal. This, however, was her birthday gift from Courtney. As much as she loved her new blanket, she would have traded it for Peanut in a heartbeat.

Never showing up last night, Tora just figured Courtney and Ben had made up. She shot her a quick text before heading for bed to which Courtney replied, "Talk to you tomorrow." Courtney could be a handful, but Ben always had a way of calming her down.

She never got the opportunity to ask Jill about her husband's remark, and she never got to hear what Jill was going to tell her last night. Courtney called and interrupted it all. On top of everything, she then had the balls to not show up.

Lying in bed, Tora was alone with her thoughts and missing her adorable, four-legged friend. That frisky little Peanut would have been trying to hop onto the bed and lay beside Tora, if she wasn't there already.

Missing her tiny face and the way her innocent little brown eyes would look at her, Tora felt a piece of her was missing. Love, loyalty, and the wagging of her teeny tail in excitement as she greeted Tora at the door each day, was an instant cure for whatever ailed her.

Peanut was a welcomed change and Tora hadn't changed things much after Dane left. While he wasn't there in body, he'd been there in hygiene products and home accessories.

Jill, another welcomed change, made her get rid of those things. Instrumental in helping her get over Dane, Jill opened a new world for Tora. Together they shared funny moments in each other's marriages. They spoke about the crazy things that go on inside one's head, the things you don't share with just anyone. They confided in each other about life and what scared them. Happy times in their lives as well as sad, along with other things women talked about that men wouldn't understand.

That was enough thinking; it was time to get up. Reaching for her robe at the foot of her bed, she slipped it on. She made her bed, fluffed her pillows, and when she turned, Tora saw herself in her mirrored closet.

Unraveling the tie of her robe, she opened it wide. In pink panties and matching tank top, Tora noticed how her figure had changed since she began eating better and exercising with Jill. Tora was transforming. Her waist curved in and her thighs no longer touched. There was some tightening, and her stomach looked a little flatter. Even her breasts seemed to have some lift.

Tora hadn't felt this good about her reflection or herself for quite some time. She must have been sleeping better, too. Her hair didn't have its usual tousled bird's nest look. Closing her robe, she walked to the kitchen to make her daily cup of tea. It was Saturday, and she was off. Today was a good day, a good day to be Tora.

Walking to her large window, she wrapped her hands around the warm mug and sipped her hot tea. The early autumn view from her bay window just added to her feeling of contentment. Sitting on the window seat, watching the leaves twist and spin along the ground, she felt good. Tora was now beginning to understand what Jill meant about the freedoms of living alone as she began to embrace it herself.

In the distance, Tora could hear her cell phone ringing. Following the sound back to her bedroom, it was Courtney's name displayed on the caller ID. Her sister had some nerve calling her so early in the morning, especially after being a no-show last night.

"Hello." she said flatly.

"Oh, Tora!" Courtney cried out.

Bracing herself for bad news, Tora placed her teacup gently on her nightstand and sat on her bed. "What is it? What's wrong!"

"It's Peanut! The vet is coming here. I'm afraid to move her!"

"I'm on my way!"

Immediately ending the call, Tora stood up and pulled the first thing she found from her closet. Slipping on black leggings and a bulky purple sweater, she hurried to the bathroom. Vigorously brushing her teeth, she splashed water on her face. She'd never worked so fast to get herself together in her life.

Grabbing her purse from the hook and squishing her feet inside the first pair sneakers she saw, she bolted out the door, jumped into her car and raced off to Courtney's.

If it was something bad, Tora wouldn't be able to forgive herself for not insisting on keeping Peanut after becoming so attached. She felt the same as the morning of Dane's accident, responsible and to blame. Was Peanut, ... she couldn't bear the thought of something so terrible.

Pulling up behind a gray Audi in the driveway, Tora jumped out. Racing up the stone steps, she pushed through Courtney's large double glass doors and followed the sound of her sister's voice.

Courtney, Ben, and another man, who Tora assumed was the vet, hovered over Peanut. Tora could see her motionless little body lying limp on her princess bed, in what looked like a tiny ballerina outfit, stuffed arms coming around and over her head.

"How ridiculous," Tora thought to herself. Maybe Peanut wasn't sick, just embarrassed. "I came as fast as I could! How is she?"

Peanut's little head suddenly bobbed up, then she rose up on all fours. Little ballet legs hanging from her costume made it appear as if she were doing a bourrée ballet move as she shuffled across the freshly polished ceramic floor tiles.

Tora held out her arms as Peanut jumped as high as she could. Bending over to catch her, Peanut jumped into Tora's hands and began licking Tora's face, trying to wrap her tiny paws around her at the same time.

The vet, holding a small stethoscope, looked at Courtney and Ben, whose jaws dropped to see Peanut so full of energy.

Ben threw his arms up in the air. "It's a miracle!" he joked.

"My work here's done." The man concluded, placing his items back in his black leather medical bag.

The vet was young, but his black-framed glasses made him look older than he was. She could see he had a good build under his blue button-down dress shirt, which was untucked from his blue jeans. He looked unprofessionally stylish, comfortable. He had a nice face which Tora took notice of.

"That's it?" Courtney asked, disappointed, as if she had just been under served at her favorite restaurant.

"False alarm. I think she just missed -" hesitating, the vet looked over at Tora.

"I'm her sister Tora," she smiled.

"Matteo," he introduced, giving an old-fashioned gentlemanly head bow.

"She was depressed. So, what does that mean, she needs medication?" Courtney gasped.

"No medication. I think she will be fine," Matteo replied, giving Peanut a little pet on the head.

Looking over at her sister, Tora saw a look she never had before plastered across her sister's face. For once, Courtney lost something to Tora, something she had no control over.

"Well, it's obvious," Courtney announced with a flick of her hair. "Peanut will have to go home with Tora."

Making it sound more like punishment, Courtney was acting like a spoiled brat. As usual, she dictated how it would be without checking first. Only this time Tora didn't mind.

"Okay." Tora quickly agreed.

"I'd love to follow up with a few house calls," Matteo offered, turning his attention back to Tora.

"I would appreciate that," she smiled graciously.

"I'd love to see Peanut in that environment, just to make sure all is well, and this isn't just a fluke."

Tora knew it wasn't a fluke. It was obvious to everyone Matteo was trying to spare Courtney's feelings, except Courtney.

"I have a hair appointment at twelve," Courtney then announced. "I will pack up her items right now. Ben, grab the bed," she barked.

"I've got it," Matteo said, jumping at the opportunity to help.

As Courtney stepped three feet in either direction, she collected Peanuts items and placed them carefully in a pink doggy duffle bag. This one had Peanuts name and face emblazoned across the front.

Taking the bag from Courtney, Matteo then lifted the lightweight bed, and they all walked to the front door.

"I'll get her clothes together during the week." Courtney informed her sister.

Clothes, Tora laughed to herself. Peanut had a better wardrobe than she did.

"And her furniture." Courtney added cold as a stone.

"Do you want to say goodbye?" She asked, holding Peanut out at arm's length.

Hesitating, Courtney shot her sister an icy look. "Goodbye."

"That's my sister." Tora whispered to the vet as they walked out to her car together.

Tora was overjoyed Peanut was all right and back in her arms. Following the vet outside, she led him to her car.

Lifting his arms, "I can put this stuff in my trunk," Matteo offered, smiling an uneven smile that rose higher on the left than it did on the right.

Having read once a crooked smile had something to do with one's brain, Tora found it attractive as opposed to flawed. And as much as she wanted to say yes to this handsome doctor, following her home may not be a good idea. She'd just met this man and had no idea how long Courtney had known him either.

Besides, if he were really interested, he would make sure he kept his word about that follow-up visit.

"Maybe stop by next week?" she asked. "I'm thinking of setting Peanut's stuff up, taking her for a nice walk and spending a little one on one-time. We need to catch up. I missed this little fur ball," she said in a baby voice, giving

Peanut a gentle squeeze, showering her with kisses atop her head.

While Tora secured Peanut in her rear passenger doggy seat, Matteo placed the bag and bed in Tora's trunk. Meeting her at the driver's side, Matteo closed her door as she slid behind the wheel.

Resting his hands on the car door, leaning his head in a bit, "Please don't hesitate to call me if Peanut starts to act funny or lethargic again." He flashed that one-sided smile of his once more, as if he knew Tora liked it.

"I don't think that will happen," she replied confidently, when inside she was slowly turning to putty.

"Neither do I."

"Thank you so very much, Doc." *Doc?* Where did that come from? Was that too comfortable she wondered?

"Tora?"

She liked his voice and the way it sounded when he said her name. He had her attention.

"Let's have dinner tonight." he suggested out of the blue.

Her heart thumped. Did she hear him correctly? Dinner? Tonight?

"I would like to get to know you. What do you think?"

Tora wanted to scream *Yes! Yes! Yes!* But hid her enthusiasm well.

Grinning from ear to ear, Matteo reached into the back pocket of his jeans and pulled out his business card. "Text me. We can take it from there," he said politely, then handed it to Tora.

Taking the card, "Until then." she agreed.

Giving her car door a tap of his hand, Matteo took a step back.

Tora started her car and proceeded to back up out of the driveway. As she pointed her car toward home, Tora checked her rear-view mirror where she could see Matteo, now standing at the foot of her sister's driveway. She felt bad not allowing him to come along. He seemed so nice. If it were meant to be, they would see each other tonight.

"Oh, my gosh Peanut! Doc wants to go to dinner!" She squealed in delight, glancing back at Peanut, safely secured in her doggy seat. The stuffed ballet hands above her head bounced around like two antennas. The feet sticking out of the costume below her neck made Tora feel sorry for this little pooch. A nice collar, cute sweater, maybe, but a costume? As cute and funny as it looked, it was demeaning. "Don't worry Peanut, no more costumes for you."

Feeling a jolt in her jacket pocket, she slid out her cell phone to see who it was. *Text message* her phone read. It was from Dane. What timing. At first her curiosity peeked, then she didn't give a shit and shoved her phone back in her pocket. She had more important things on her mind.

Chapter
15

The blue jeans she chose fit perfectly. Her plain cranberry knit sweater went well with her long blonde hair. A black belt and her heeled black boots with a swipe of rust lipstick finished her look. Tora hadn't dressed for another man in a long time. There was a nervous energy about it all that made it fun. She felt like a teenager again.

Then, a sudden wave of insecurity passed over her as she began to worry about what to talk about. Tora was never much of a talker on dates in her single years, often giving off the impression she wasn't interested. It was effortless with Dane though. The two had gotten along so well, she had plenty to say on the few dates they went on. Before she could catch her breath, they got engaged. Soon after they married. She hoped the conversation would be as easy with Matteo.

Almost ready to leave, Tora checked to make sure she had locked the windows and turned off the stove for one last time.

She then went to her bedroom to check on Peanut who was lying on her princess bed fast asleep.

"I'm sorry I'm seeing Doc without you," she whispered. "I'll be back soon," feeling guilty as she tiptoed out of the house.

Getting into her car, she could not help but feel quilty sneaking off and leaving Peanut at home by herself. It was as if she had something to hide. Sort of like two friends who hit it off and go out one night without the rest of the group. It feels wrong; you feel bad, but sometimes you enjoy a little one on one.

Don't talk about Dane. Don't talk about the affair. She kept repeating this over and over to herself so many times as she got into the car. Now she worried she may do the opposite of what she was telling herself not to. Why were first dates so hard?

They planned to meet at The Bistro. A cute little outdoor café on Main Street in the next town over, only minutes away from her home. Against Matteo's wishes, Tora insisted on meeting him there. If the date was a dud, she had her own car, could feign sickness and get the heck out of there. Knowing she had an escape took the edge off.

It also eliminated the awkwardness of saying good night afterward. How was one to know when it was a good time to get out of the car? How long do you sit and chat, and is it rude not to invite him in. Then there's the old *I'll call you.* Before exiting, do you hug, do you kiss? At thirty-five years old, who wanted to play guessing games.

Feeling like she could have used more time to loosen up and talk to herself in the car, she had arrived. Why was it the more anxious you were, the faster it seemed you would get to where you were going?

Easily finding a parking spot, Tora pulled in and shut the engine. It was show time. Getting out of her car, she pressed the button on her key fob to lock it, then dropped it in her purse.

Walking toward the restaurant, she could see Matteo seated on the outdoor patio, faced in the opposite direction. She was relieved. Otherwise, it would have been nerve-wracking for her to walk toward him. What if she tripped, or her boot heel caught a crack, causing her to misstep, or worse - what if she fell? Oh, the things Tora worried about.

"Hello stranger!" Tora exclaimed. Bracing herself with her hands, her feet left the floor as she leaned in over the railing that separated the restaurant from the street. Tora was in a playful mood catching not only Matteo by surprise, but herself as well.

Poking his face out instinctively to give her a kiss but stopped and withdrew.

"I'll be right in." Planting her feet back on the ground, Tora made her way to the entrance.

Walking through the crowded eatery, Tora turned heads, including Matteo's. He did not take his eyes off her once she was back in his sight.

Standing, Matteo pulled out her seat.

"Thank you," she said sweetly as she took her seat. Matteo pushed her chair in and sat back down.

"You catch a guy's eye."

Tora smiled a shy, bashful smile. It was very nice of him to say whether he meant it or not. Compliments were what a woman needed to hear every so often. Dane had rarely given them.

Matteo looked different tonight. He wasn't wearing his glasses, giving him less of a scholarly look, and his smooth face now had a hint of five o'clock shadow. She still found him just as appealing, if not more.

"I hope you don't mind; I ordered a bottle of wine. I thought one small glass?"

"Sure." Taking her glass in hand, she held it up for him to pour.

Filling their glasses halfway, he rested the bottle down on the table, "To our first night out," Matteo said, raising his glass.

First night out? She preferred *first date*, but she liked the sound of it anyway. "To our first night out."

Clicking their glasses, they sipped and gazed into each other's eyes. If she didn't know better, one may say he was nervous himself. Maybe more nervous than her.

"Did Peanut give the thumbs up for tonight?" he asked.

"She sure did."

"I think she likes me."

"I know she likes you."

"I really admired what you did today."

"What did I do?" Tora had no idea what Matteo was referring to.

"Without hesitation, you agreed to take Peanut. It was obvious she missed you. I just didn't have the heart to tell your sister, but it was plain to see when Peanut's behavior changed as soon as she saw you."

"My sister got Peanut at a time in my life that really made a difference. She stayed with me while Courtney was away, who by the way had only had her for one day," then she caught herself. It was rude to speak ill of her selfish sister. That wasn't Tora's way, and she didn't want to give the wrong impression. "I even felt bad leaving her home tonight. I'm so attached."

"I can see why she was so happy to see you today. I was happy to see you walk into the room tonight. So happy, I almost ran across the floor and jumped into your arms myself."

Picturing that, Tora found it comical. She teared up and almost choked on her wine.

"So," she began, regaining her composure, "Tell me, what made you become a vet? With your build I would have taken you for construction or something more physical."

"Really?" he asked, with a look of surprise, or maybe it was modesty. "Hmm, what made me become a vet?" he repeated, taking a moment to think. "We were fishing, just as we always did at my uncle's cabin. We hadn't caught anything all day. Just as we were about to pack it up, a fish caught my line. I turned to give my rod to my cousin Tim so he could reel in his very first fish and that's when I spotted it. An alligator about eight feet long was slowly creeping up behind him. I dropped the rod. I leapt over my cousin and toward the alligator as if I had wings." He exclaimed lifting his arms out. "Somehow I was able to grab the alligator in a headlock," he wrapped his burly arms around one another, rocking back and forth as if he were wrestling it right then and there.

Tora's eyes widened. "Oh, my god this story is amazing!"

"I know, it really is. It's so amazing that I can't believe it myself," he laughed, lowering his head. "I can't finish this story."

"Why not? You have to tell me the rest!"

"It's not true," shaking his head, laughing. "I made it up."

"What!" Tora laughed back, lifting her linen napkin from the table, she waved it out and snapped it at Matteo. "I believed you! You are a good storyteller."

"I could see you were really getting into it. I felt like such a liar."

Tora liked to hear that lying made him uncomfortable. Her husband had lied to her for months, maybe even years, and he didn't seem uncomfortable at all.

"Well, thanks for your honesty. Wait, was that honesty?" she questioned in jest.

Sharing another laugh, they mimicked each other as they sipped their wine followed by a sip of water. They laughed again when realizing they were doing the same thing. Just as she had hoped, they were hitting it off.

Lifting his menu, "I hope you are eating tonight. And I would like if you ordered more than a salad," Matteo said.

"Well, I was going to order a salad. Let's check it out," she said, lifting the menu she gave it a look see.

Not having much of an appetite, Tora had the flutters, as if she'd swallowed a net full of butterflies. She was enjoying his company, so much more than any entrée she could order.

Then, there were the other things. Things that could embarrass a girl. Just thinking about eating made Tora self-conscious. What if there was food in her teeth, on her lip or even worse, … her face?

Peeking out from behind her menu, she looked around the eatery. None of the other women seemed to hold back, as a matter of fact, they were digging right in.

"I have an idea." Matteo announced, clapping his menu closed.

Closing her menu also, she gave him her full attention.

"Instead of ordering from the menu, let's order something from the wall."

The wall?

The items listed on the menu were photographed, after they had been beautifully constructed, for display all along the walls. One of Tora's favorites, an eggplant tower, was there too. The stacks of eggplant, sliced tomatoes, red pepper and melted mozzarella cheese, which was dripping down along the sides looked sinfully delicious, while still leaning toward somewhat healthy. The picture alone looked edible.

"And," he added, "whatever we order tonight, let's make sure we order something, at least one thing you've never had before."

"Why? What if I don't like it?"

"I want tonight to be memorable. If you try something you never had before, you will always remember it. You will remember if you liked it, you will remember if you didn't. Either way, you will remember you ate it with me."

Stop! Stop! Stop! Tora's inner voice shouted. *Is this guy perfect or what!* Being unprepared and green as hell, that sentiment needed a comeback, a good one at that.

Leaning in, Tora looked into Matteo's eyes. "I will remember tonight. Not by what I ate, but because I am here with you."

By the expression on Matteo's face, she knew it was the perfect reply. Who was this new Tora and where had she been hiding?

"So," she said, leaning back against her chair, "what does the Doctor recommend?"

"I will have to look at the menu for this. Have you ever had -" pausing, he reopened his menu, slapping it closed again, he tossed it to the side, "grilled squid?"

"No, I have never had grilled squid. I never even heard of grilled quid."

"Well, you've definitely been missing out."

"It's that good?"

"I don't know. I've never had it myself." He smiled crookedly. "Let's try it together."

The waiter, an older fellow dressed in black, approached the table and opened his small pad. Slipping the pen out, he quickly jotted down their order: a rib eye for Matteo; the eggplant tower for Tora; and as an appetizer, the grilled squid, then he scurried off.

Tora looked around the crowded restaurant. "I've seen this place a million times and heard so much about it, yet never eaten here."

"I'm glad your first time was with me." Matteo said, then quickly turned a shade of red.

Looking at each other, they both let out a loud round of laughter.

"That was -"

"Funny," Tora said, finishing his sentence before taking another sip of her wine. "I could sit here and drink a whole bottle with you. You are great company."

"Is that a date number two?"

"Don't you mean night out number two?"

"No. I mean date."

Hearing that elated Tora. "Then it's a date number two."

It was just dinner, but for Tora, there was something exhilarating about tonight. The interest in getting to know someone new, telling them about you, listening to stories you haven't heard fifty times before. Tonight, was all about what is, and what could be.

Placing the oval white dish of grilled squid in the center of the table, "Bon appétit." The waiter said in his best French accent before he disappeared in the sea of people crowding the inside area.

For a moment, they both stared at this colorless cooked creature which Tora immediately thought of as an alien on a plate. This opaque, once oblong tube was sliced in rings, two sets of tentacles rested on each side, with two lemon wedges veiled in a green net that garnished the dish.

She failed to hold in her laughter, "We eat this?"

Looking up at each other and back down at the plate before them, they didn't know what to make of it.

"Let's dig in." Lifting the serving spoon, Matteo scooped up a few slices and placed them on Tora's plate. "Legs?" he asked, scooping up the tentacles he placed them to her dish.

"Legs," Tora confirmed, as Matteo served up this deep-water delight.

Both taking a taste, they fixated on each other as they chewed and chewed.

"What do you think?" Matteo asked.

Tora bobbed her head back and forth. "A little chewy." Wishing she could spit this gum like gob right into her napkin.

"Maybe we should have squeezed the lemon on it? Definitely something to remember."

"Oh, I'll remember. I'll remember not to order this again," she giggled through the rubbery mouthful.

For the rest of the night the two chatted, continued to laugh and enjoy their meals together. Tora shared her best teacher/student stories, while Matteo shared a few funny veterinarian stories. Keeping it light, they didn't dig too deep into their own personal history. That would be best left for another night.

As the busboy cleared the dishes, the place began to empty.

"I guess we should go?" Matteo wondered aloud, looking around the empty restaurant.

"No," Tora frowned, "but yes," she sighed.

Standing, Matteo pulled out Tora's seat like a gentleman. Once she stood up, Matteo slipped his hand into hers. Leading her through the restaurant, they walked out onto the lamp post lit sidewalk of this quaint little village.

Giving his hand a little tug, Tora steered him in the direction of her car. Gently sliding her hand from Matteo's, she reached into her purse. Lifting out her key fob, she pressed the button causing her headlights to flash, unlocking her car. They walked to the driver's side and Tora leaned against the door.

"I had a great time Tora." Matteo said with smooth confidence in his voice. A glimmer from the streetlights lit up his eyes to the lightest of blues. She could easily get lost in eyes like his.

"I did too." She spoke softly.

It wasn't the wine, but they both seemed a little tipsy.

"I hope we can do this again very soon," he said, his gaze intense.

"Me too."

"I'll call you?"

"Please do."

Matteo placed his hands upon Tora's narrow waist. Slipping his thumbs through the belt loops of her jeans, he walked his body towards her. Their lips met.

Tora closed her eyes. Wanting to pull him closer, feel the weight of his body against hers, she refrained. Their kiss lingered for a moment, then they slowly parted ways.

"I'll call you," he said, releasing his hold.

Tora felt euphoric. Her eyelids were heavy, and she seemed a bit dazed. Giving Matteo a small smile, she floated into her car.

Matteo stepped back onto the sidewalk and waited as she started the engine.

As she drove away, Tora watched him disappear in her rear-view mirror as she turned the corner.

What a night, what a man and what a meal. Except for the squid, she wasn't a fan. But he was right, no matter what she thought of the squid, she would remember tonight. Always.

Chapter

16

Donna loved a good story, so when Tora agreed to have coffee after work, she jumped at the chance.

Tora set up her own cute little bistro in the sunroom next to her dining room. She'd snipped flowers from her garden earlier that morning and placed them in small vases on the table.

The view today was stunning. Fallen leaves of red, pink, orange and yellow lay scattered all along the ground, surrounding the glass-enclosed porch. Tall trees swayed in the breeze overhead and the sun peeked through the branches. It was as if someone had dropped the room in the middle of a forest.

Dane had been texting Tora last night and then again in the morning. Having no interest in what he had to say, she deleted them. She was on a high, a Matteo high, and she didn't want anyone or anything bringing her down.

"So, tell me all about it," Donna said with great interest, sitting back in her chair. "I mean, I'm not getting any action, but I'm glad one of us is."

Tora made a goofy face. That question made her uncomfortable. "Action? We just had dinner."

"C-Mon', this isn't your first rodeo. Did he do something to turn you off? Did he do something disgusting?"

Moving around the silverware on the table, "Don't ruin this for me." Tora cautioned.

"Okay, so how did it go? Tell me all about it."

"It was really nice."

Donna's eyes slid back and forth like those cat clocks with the famous rolling eyes and wagging tail. "Nice? That's it? That's all you got?" she complained with a smirk, while sipping her coffee as though this get together was a waste of her time.

"It was. What can I say? I was happy with the way I looked, and he looked fantastic. He said all the right things, but I have no expectations. It was only one date."

Tora was lying, she had expectations. Matteo seemed too perfect for her to feel any other way.

She was lucky to have met him at a time they both were single, and Courtney flippantly got a dog. Tora was enjoying this new time in her life and how it was unfolding.

"Good job, good body, good looking, so what's wrong with him?" Her husky ex- smoker voice laughed. "You better make sure he doesn't have a girlfriend, or a wife tucked away somewhere."

That comment reminded her of her own husband, and it felt like a dig.

"So, no sex." Donna's interrogation continued.

"No. No sex."

"Pfft."

"You really know how to take the romance out of it. Don't sully the night."

"Ooh, look at Miss Fancy words—sully," Donna taunted.

"G'day ladies!" Ali cheerfully greeted in a mock Australian accent, letting herself in through Tora's back glass sliding doors.

Thank goodness Ali arrived. Tora was in dire need of a buffer. "Hi Ali. I brewed coffee today. It's in the kitchen," Tora greeted, hoping to break up the tension.

"Perfect." Ali said, giving Tora a quick hug and an upward nod to Donna before disappearing inside.

"So, what's next, sex?"

"You are aware you're taking the pizzazz away?" Tora groaned.

"Taking the pizzazz away?" Donna scoffed. "I thought SEX was the PIZZAZZ!" her hoarse voice laughed. "Givem' something to come back for. Isn't that what you and your sister say?"

"Always leavem' wanting more," Tora corrected, after taking a moment to think about it herself. "You can be so disgusting sometimes. You think like a man."

"What's happening here?" Ali asked, rejoining the girls in the sunroom, she sat, coffee in hand.

"My date went great last night," Tora melted into her chair. "And Donna," she said, turning toward her, "is trying to fuck it up for me."

Tora rarely cursed, but Donna really knew how to push her buttons sometimes.

"Don't you mean I'm sullying it," she mocked in a high-class tone lifting her pinky finger as she raised her coffee mug. "I'm just being truthful," she said, loudly slurping her coffee. "Eventually this guy will want sex Tora."

Shaking her head, Tora began to rethink this get together. Donna, as colorful and entertaining as she could be, possessed a knack for shitting all over everything.

"What is it with you and the sex? We just met."

"Donna's a slut," Ali joked.

"You're killing this whole thing for me. I could have sat here today, by myself, enjoying this cloud I'm on. But noooo. Instead, I agree to put on coffee and put up with you."

"I'm sorry, I'm a realist. This is life. You have to admit, it's pretty funny."

"Not to me."

Tora's phone began to vibrate, she looked over and saw Matteo's name appear on the display.

"It's him!" she blurted out like a giddy teenager. Jumping up, she grabbed the phone and waved it over her head. "I guess I did leavem' wanting more," she sassed, childishly sticking her tongue out at Donna.

"What's up, Doc?" Donna's loudness filled the room.

Wanting privacy, Tora ducked inside the house. Donna was embarrassing. She dreaded the day these two would ever meet.

"Hi." Tora answered, trying not to sound as thrilled as she was that he'd called.

"I had a great time last night."

The sound of his voice soothed her. What did it matter what Donna thought? Her thoughts on men, or anything for that matter, were as useless as her dating website memberships.

"Me too," Tora said, twirling a lock of her hair in her fingers.

"I'd like to make that house call tonight. I'll bring a bottle of wine, so you don't have to drive this time and you can have more than one glass."

"Sounds good," Tora replied, trying not to sound overzealous.

"Around seven?"

"Seven it is.'

"See you tonight."

"See you tonight," Tora paused before ending the call, hoping she would hear his voice one more time before he hung up.

"Hang up Tora," she could hear him laugh through the phone.

"No, you hang up," she chortled back.

"I'm only hanging up because I have patients waiting. If I was home, I'd keep you on this phone until you cried uncle."

"Okay, okay. I don't want to keep you from your furry patients. I will see you tonight."

"Thank you."

"You are welcome. Goodbye," she finally said and hung up. Spinning around, she let out a shriek. It was official!

Matteo had a great time last night and wanted to see her as soon as possible. Tora was walking on air and not even Donna had the power to change that.

Rejoining the ladies at the table, Donna smiled shrewdly raising her brow. "You're seeing him tonight."

"He's making a house call."

Donna let out a hardy laugh. "House call? Don't you mean booty call?" She continued laughing to the point of almost coughing. "There's that sex I told you about." sounding so sure of herself.

Donna had been on a few dates herself with the help of her online dating addiction, but no luck. She wasn't exactly the easiest person to get along with. She had a toughness about her that protected her and her fragile interior. Deep down, Donna was a sensitive mush who felt empowered by raining on parades. Just like today.

"Where is he taking you?" Donna asked suspiciously.

"We're staying here."

"Oh boy! He's a cheapskate. No doubt about it. Head for the hills my friend!"

Tora just rolled her eyes up and down. Why was Donna being such a bitch to her today?

"Isn't he a doctor?" Donna asked, continuing her harassment.

"A vet." Ali corrected.

"Is that like a chiropractor? People call them Doctor, but are they?" Donna asked, shooting Ali a side look. Ruffling feathers and chipping away at their friendship at the same time, Donna was a real multi-tasker.

If Jill were here, she would have shut her down in a heartbeat.

"You've got him excited. I'm telling you. Your house, a bottle of wine ..." Donna teased.

As much as Tora tried to ignore it, Donna was steadily getting on her nerves. She thought it was funny, but it wasn't funny to Tora as she poured it on a little thicker than usual.

"Why don't you finish your coffee and go," Tora suggested. "Now."

Donna's lids snapped back. "Are you throwing me out?"

"Don't you have some babies to make cry. Some villages to burn." Tora had enough.

Donna grinned with satisfaction. "I'll stop. I don't want to make you mad. You know me, I can't help it. I have issues."

"You should talk to somebody about that."

Faking a smile, Tora continued to drink her coffee. Had everything reached its expiration? First her marriage, and now her friendships? She wondered why she was even trying to make this work. Was it her? Was it them? Eh, what did it matter? All she could think about was seeing Matteo tonight.

"Does Dane know you're seeing someone?" Ali curiously asked.

The wound slowly healing now felt picked at. "I don't know," Tora replied with a who cares kind of attitude, "but he has a girlfriend, and that's okay because I'm moving on."

Ali and Donna looked at each other skeptically.

"I don't think I would have been as calm as you. I mean seeing what you saw, in the hospital that morning." Ali stated.

Ali was jumping on the bandwagon. It took nerve for her to bring that up. The morning that exposed her husband for the man he had hid well, or not so well, for the last five years.

"I used to think about that. Should I have asked questions, made a scene? The more I thought about it, the more I'm sure I did the right thing."

"The right thing? You did nothing," Donna bitterly pointed out.

"Exactly," she said, looking at Donna. "What was there to do? Fight for a cheating husband? I have more respect for myself than that."

"Anything would have been better than leaving with your tail between your legs."

That stung. Why was Donna attacking her, and so viciously? Besides, who was the victim here?

"I haven't told you, but you are looking fabulous," Ali blurted out. "Whatever you are doing is paying off," she smiled.

It felt good to hear someone other than herself had noticed the work she had put into herself. It was even nicer of Ali to say it at that moment. Tora was thankful Ali had changed the subject, just as Tora had done for her so many times before.

"Now *I* need to lose some weight." Donna said, grabbing the flab that hung over her pants with her two hands and squeezing tight, "and I need to find a chiropractor. This gut of mine is wreaking havoc on my back." She laughed. "Or maybe a plastic surgeon. I'd love a tummy tuck."

"We should all just eat greener," Ali suggested.

"Green?" Donna asked. "You mean like grass?" She laughed, cracking herself up as usual.

"Yes, green. For example, a green salad with dinner instead of potatoes."

"Oh, but potatoes sound so good. Mashed, with lots of butter," Donna said, almost salivating.

"Broccoli, spinach, stuff like that." Tora added between sips from her mug.

"If you say Kale …" Donna playfully pointed her finger at Tora.

"Kale," Tora laughed. "No really, let's eat greener. I like that Ali."

As mean spirited as Donna could be, Tora found it hard to stay mad. She knew Donna, just like herself at one time, was not happy with a lot of things going on in her life. Food being one of them.

"You're not brainwashing me! Or in this case— greenwashing. I'm not having it!" Donna protested.

"It's called eating right and taking care of yourself. You don't agree with anything. Ever." Tora argued. "You sit here and complain you don't like certain things but refuse to do anything to change it."

Donna chugged down her coffee and stood. She lifted her designer bag from the back of her seat and let out a big sigh. "I gotta go, but if you want me over tomorrow after your booty call tonight, I'm gonna need a bagel."

"Green!" Tora reminded Donna, who sashayed toward the patio door like a model on the runway.

"All right! With scallion cream cheese then!" She shot back.

"Bye Dee!" Ali called out.

After the door closed, Ali stood. "Everything you say to Donna gets back to Dane. I just wanted you to know. Please keep that between us," she said, walking to a seated Tora. "I'm gonna go too." leaning over to she gave Tora a quick hug. "You have fun tonight." She winked.

"Bye Al," she said, as Ali exited the sunroom. Closing the door behind her, she gave Tora a friendly wave through the glass and down the stone path leading to the front of Tora's home.

Tora paid attention to what she'd just heard. She now had to filter her conversations with Donna. Her life was not Dane's business.

But none of that mattered. Tora was preoccupied with seeing Matteo tonight. Yes, he was bringing a bottle of wine. Yes, they would be alone, so Tora had to think. What if one thing led to another? She needed a plan; she needed to be prepared. How far was too far, and how far wasn't far enough? Should she shave her legs, just in case?

Chapter

17

On the coffee table was a large white tray filled with a variety of cheese, crackers and a bunch of grapes smack dead in the center.

"There, at least we'll have something to pick on," Tora said aloud to herself as she admired her handy work.

What if Donna was right and Matteo was a cheapskate? He didn't look it, but then again, what does a cheapskate look like? He was such a nice guy, but nice guys could be cheap too. She just didn't take him for being tight with a buck, then again, they'd just met. Tora doubted anything would surprise her anymore.

"No cheese for you," Tora warned Peanut over the kitchen counter. She'd been eyeballing the cheese plate ever since Tora set it down. Rushing back to her bed, she circled on top before finding a spot to drop into.

The chiming of the doorbell got Peanut springing to her feet and darting for the door. Instead of barking, Peanut stood there waiting.

Tora could see Matteo's image through the glass. She noticed how Peanut seemed to know who it was just by the ringing of the doorbell.

Tora opened the door with excitement, "Hello!" she cheerfully greeted with a smile that ran from ear to ear.

Matteo stood there, smiling wide himself, with a thick plastic bag held at his side. "Wine." He said, holding up the bag he stepped inside.

"That's the magic word." Tora joked, closing the door behind them and locking it.

As Matteo walked in, Peanut gave his ankle a sniff and ran back off to the comfort of her bed.

"Right this way." Tora said, leading Matteo to the kitchen.

Opening the cabinet, Tora pulled out two wine glasses and a long black bottle opener.

"I was going to ask you to dinner, but by the time I left the clinic and showered, I thought it would be too late to eat." Matteo said as he lifted the bottles from the bag one by one, standing them on the counter. "You don't look like you're a late-night eater, anyway." Matteo commented while Tora, holding back a smile, used the electric bottle opener to uncork one of the three bottles of red wine Matteo had brought.

"Do you plan on drinking a lot tonight?" she asked, pouring wine into their glasses.

Balling up the empty bag, Matteo gave a sly grin. "Maybe, and if we get hungry, we could always order Chinese. Chow's in the village is pretty good. I have them in my contacts."

Maybe he wasn't cheap after all. Inside, Tora was on top of the world. Why was she letting Donna put ideas in her head? There were things way worse than being cheap anyway, like cheating, but it wasn't the time or place to let her thoughts wander down that dark road.

"A man with a plan. I like that."

Taking the plastic bag from his hand, she tossed it in the corner of the counter and lifted the wine glasses.

"For you." She smiled, handing Matteo his glass.

Taking it, "Thank you." he said.

Together they walked into the dimly lit living room and sat at opposite ends of the sofa. Tora had not been home alone with a man other than Dane, ever. Well, there was that one time their mother left both her and her sister home to go to the movies and the neighbor boy, Jimmy Breslin, came by selling chocolates for their local church. Courtney eagerly invited him in. It still amused Tora to this day, remembering how fancy and grown up her sister acted, as she asked questions about the different types of candy and what was in them, like she was some sort of a chocolatier. The things you do when your young.

Tora watched as Matteo sat back and relaxed. He had a presence about him, making the energy in the room come alive, just from him being in it. Taking a deep breath, he turned his body toward Tora. She enjoyed seeing him look so comfortable in her home.

Matteo smiled that smile of his. "I don't want you to think I'm cheap."

"Cheap," Tora laughed. "I don't think that." Little did he know.

"I just wanted to be alone and talk."

"Here we are." She raised her glass and took a sip.

"Did you always live in Bucks Falls?"

Uh, oh. This could be trouble. She didn't want to talk about Dane or their marriage, but it looked like that's right where it was heading.

"No. I started out in New York."

"How did you end up here?"

"It's a long, boring story. Nothing worth talking about tonight, that's for sure. How about you, were you always a Bucks resident?"

"So, your story is long and boring, but mine isn't?"

"Nope. Yours isn't boring to me."

Matteo looked sincerely interested in anything she was willing to share. That caused Tora to feel pressure. The pressure to say the right thing, pressure to not come off as Tora Bora.

"Ok. I'll play along," he obliged. "I'm originally from Pittsburgh. I went to school in Colorado. Once I graduated, my parents helped me open my practice."

"What do your parents do?"

"My mom was, and still is a stay at-home-mom. To my dad that is," he joked. "She continues to do all that mom stuff. Only now it's for my dad"

Tora knew about that mom stuff all too well, and she didn't even have any kids.

"My dad, he had a school uniform business that really took off. He made a small fortune from his office in our basement."

"Smart man."

"It's all about the timing if you ask me. He had the cash to help me open a small office here, and as my patient list grew, I was able to pay my parents back. Eventually, the space became too small, and I bought the building next door to expand my practice. It would have been perfect if my parents hadn't had to help me financially. Money, it makes such a difference. How would I have ever opened my own practice, especially with student loans?"

Talking about it seemed to stress Matteo. "It reminds me, I have to call my parents. I should visit them soon."

"How far are they?"

"Still in Pittsburgh, they still live in my childhood home. Maybe you'll take a ride out with me one day," he said casually. "You can see all the geeky stuff I used to collect."

Meet the parents? Tora almost choked on her wine. This was absurdly fast. She knew he was too good to be true, but after hearing this, something had to be wrong.

Oh, stop it Tora, maybe he didn't mean it like that, or maybe he was just being polite.

"I'm up for a road trip," she blurted out, thinking it probably wouldn't happen anyway.

Smiling, Matteo took a sip of his wine. "You asked me why I became a vet the other night. I didn't answer your question."

"It's all right. You don't have to tell me," she said. There were some questions she didn't want to answer herself. If he didn't want to answer that question when she first asked, he must have had his reasons.

"I will tell you. It's good to talk about," he said, adjusting himself in a story telling position on the sofa. "I had a dog when I was a kid. Her name was Skye. One day, Skye couldn't walk anymore. Back then, people rarely took their dogs to the vet. I mean, sure, some people did, but not my parents. Finally, when it got too much to keep bringing Skye in and out to avoid a mess in the house, my dad took her to get looked at. She had cancer."

Tora winced. It made sense to her now, why Matteo made up that outrageous story the other night and didn't tell her the real reason he chose his profession. It was sad. Tora knew it would not end well, and she hoped she wouldn't cry. Thank goodness she was only on her first glass of wine. Winey and weepy was not a good look for her.

"And the funny thing is when I would pet her, I could feel the lumps all along her underbelly. I was so young, about seven years old. I didn't know what I was feeling was cancer." His cute uneven smile now hung long as a fiddle. "We never got her fixed, if she had been, she probably wouldn't have gotten that type of cancer. The vet, being an animal lover, helped take away the pain by putting Skye to sleep."

Tora's eyes began to well up and she fought hard to keep the pooling contained. She wanted to say something to change the subject or ease his pain, but she had no idea what.

"It was hard for my dad. I remember him coming home without her. My mom knew and just hugged him when he came back. I was supposed to be in bed asleep, but I waited for them both. When I got up the next day, no one said a word and I never asked. Since I saw my dad come home without Skye, I just knew she wasn't coming back. I had no idea where he took her or why, but that was my seven-year-old mind."

"Skye. What a beautiful name."

"She had the bluest eyes, and her coat was white, like a cloud."

"I'm so sorry, Matteo."

"That's the sad thing about pets. They die. The same thing with people. We all leave eventually, for one reason or another," he said, looking up at the ceiling, giving a little laugh, "whether we want to or not." He looked back at Tora. "I can't even imagine my parents dying. Not being able to pick up the phone and say hi to my mother and talk to my dad about the Phillies. That's enough about me, how about your parents Tora? Are they still with you?"

"My dad is dead," she blurted out, "and my mom is in New York. Thank you for answering my question by the way." She smiled sweetly, dabbing the corners of her eyes with her knuckles. "Again, you brought me to tears," she joked, remembering how she laughed till she cried that night at the restaurant. "I feel I should answer your other question though. What brought me here."

As much as Tora did not want to talk about her husband or her marriage, she felt she owed it to Matteo to be truthful. She had nothing to hide, and the subject would come up sooner or later if they continued seeing each other. Why not rip the band aid off right now?

"I was here visiting my sister from New York and her friend was catering a party. One of the staff called out sick, so my sister asked me if I wanted to make a few extra bucks. I was on summer break from working as a teacher, so I was happy to make the extra cash. That's where I met my husband, and what started out as a long-distance relationship," she said and threw her hands up. "Here I am."

"Thank you for that." He bowed his head appreciatively. "Which leads me to another question." Matteo then edged his way over a little closer to Tora. "I like you Tora. I know it hasn't been that long since you and your husband separated."

Thanks, Courtney.

"Is there any chance of you and …"

"Dane." she replied, helping him fill in the blank.

"Like the dog?"

Tora snorted, "Yes, like the dog."

"We just met so if there is any chance you and Dane may get back together, I would appreciate you being honest with me. I'd like to know if this …" he said, pointing his finger back and forth between the two of them, "us," he corrected. "If we have a chance here."

"Dane and I will not get back together. Ever." She assured him.

Matteo smiled. "We just started seeing each other. I don't want to scare you off. I just think it's fair that if we spend time together, which by the way," he smiled and took her hand, "I love spending time with you. I don't want to step on another guy's toes, and I definitely don't want to get in the way of a possible reconciliation."

Tora knew there was no way of that ever happening and wanted to assure Matteo of that.

"I get it. Believe me, I really do. Ever been married yourself?"

"Nope. Came close. She cheated—with my best friend," he said, withdrawing to his side of the couch.

Everyone had someone who did a number on them it seemed.

"Any chance of getting back with her?" Tora asked, circling the rim of her wineglass with her finger.

"First of all, they're married, so no. Plus, it seemed to have worked for them. Maybe they were meant to be. I'm not mad anymore. They even have kids."

"You're still in touch?"

"No. Mutual friends, they tell me stuff. I'm happy for them. The guys miss the trips we used to take. I miss the trips too. They probably hope we'll get passed it one day, or rather, I get passed it," he half laughed. "I am passed it. I just don't think I could ever take a trip with him."

Hearing Matteo speak made her wonder why her own friends didn't seem to miss her like his friends missed him? "We'd been planning our last trip before the big guy break up." he joked.

"To where?"

"A couple of the guys wanted to go to New Orleans for Madi Gras. We hadn't decided on a place. Just the planning got our blood pumping. It's always nice to have something to look forward to. Good times that I will never forget, but that part of my life is over," he said with finality.

"At least your friends wanted to keep you involved. My friends don't seem to care, and they have no compassion whatsoever."

"They are friends with your ex too?"

A look of disgust crossed Tora's face, as if she just smelled something bad. "They all grew up together."

"I'm sorry to say it, but you're probably better off. Even if it's just for the sake of moving on."

"I agree, but I lost a lot."

'Sometimes we lose things, only to find better things."

Hearing that reminded Tora of her grandmother back in North Carolina and those summers she spent there, listening to the wisdom her dear ole *Granmaw* shared.

"I like that," she said, her face appeared to illuminate from within. "So, let's see what else we have in common other than being cheated on," she joked, trying to make light of another dismal topic. "What type of movies do you like?"

"I like action. But, occasionally, more than I care to admit, I get in the mood for a good horror."

"Me too! It's hard to find a good horror now-a-day. Everything is brutal and gory."

Tora threw out a couple of B-rated horror movie titles she didn't think Matteo would have seen, but to her delight he had. They talked for hours, sipping wine while conversing about their favorites. They even made a game out of it as they tried to stump one another by naming celebrities who got their big break acting in a horror movie, while the other had to guess the name of the movie that marked their acting debut. Tora hadn't felt this engaged in a long time.

"I better go," he said as he peeked at his wristwatch, and jumped up before anything or anyone tried to persuade him differently. "It's almost eleven!"

That confused Tora. Just a few hours earlier Matteo was talking about meeting the parents; the next he was ready to run out the door. "Will you turn into a pumpkin?"

"I have early appointments tomorrow. I'm sorry to rush off like this. I totally lost track of time," he replied as he reached for his cell phone on the coffee table and pressed a few buttons.

She hoped he wasn't married. He couldn't have been. Courtney would have known, wouldn't she?

Looking at Tora, his endearing smile returned, "You distract me." he complimented.

Tora liked hearing she was a distraction. "You're not driving, are you? We drank a lot of wine."

"I took Uber here," he smiled, raising his phone. "Oktoberfest is next weekend. Would you join me?"

Tora was thrilled he was asking her to go out again. It took her worry off his abrupt departure.

"I haven't been to an Oktoberfest in a very long time."

"Is that a yes?"

"That's a yes."

Tora placed her wineglass on the table as did Matteo and rose to her feet to face him. They slowly moved their bodies closer to one another.

Matteo took her in his arms and began to kiss her passionately as they both made their way to the front door; walking and kissing, kissing and walking.

"I had another great night Tora," he said as he pulled away. There was longing in his voice.

The attraction was strong, Tora couldn't tell herself different, even if she tried. "So did I." she cooed, raising her lips to his ear, her cheek grazing his.

A slight vibration erupted in Matteo's pocket. "He's here," Matteo breathed.

"Who?"

"The Uber."

Matteo pulled away reluctantly and looked deeply into Tora's blue eyes. "I'll call you tomorrow."

Tora's hands slid down his arms, then to his hands, and down to his fingers, holding on to every moment, not wanting this night to end.

"Sweet dreams," she said, opening the door for him.

Standing in the doorway, Tora watched as Matteo walked down the pathway, stepped into his taxi, and was driven away into the lonely darkness of night.

Tora closed the door and double locked it, then leaned her back against it. More than disappointed, Tora's sensible side knew it was best to let him leave. It was just too soon to do anything more. Way too soon.

"Always gotta leavem' wanting more," she joked to herself out loud, and she was certainly wanting more. Maybe Matteo was familiar with that saying, too.

Chapter

18

"My favorite season," Tora gushed, as she walked into the festival grounds holding Peanut in one arm, tightly latched onto Matteo with the other.

"Now it's mine too," he said, giving her arm a playful yank.

"That sunset is to die for." Tora was in awe as she peered out across the field. Her eyes absorbed the beautiful orange and red sky which served as the backdrop for Everly Fields Oktoberfest.

As usual, this event drew a crowd, but to Tora it was just the three of them there tonight.

Matteo reached into his denim jacket pocket, pulled out his cell phone, and set it to camera. "Let's take a picture," he suggested, stopping them in their tracks.

"Say Pumpkin Spice!" Tora prompted as they put their heads close together raising Peanut up in the middle. Matteo repeatedly clicked pictures. "One more," he said, as their smiles changed into funny faces.

"I can't wait to see those later." Tora got a kick out of Matteo's playfulness.

Strolling arm in arm, they slowly made their way around the vendors. Going from booth to booth, they checked out what each stand had on their menu.

"Schnitzel," he said, pointing at the sign in amusement.

"Not my favorite. You should try the Bratwurst. It's a big wiener in a bun." she giggled.

"I'd say Sauerbraten is my favorite."

"I LOVE Sauerbraten! And potato pancakes! If made correctly, and not too oily."

"I know a great place. We'll have to go."

It secretly excited Tora to hear Matteo speak of plans in the future.

"Look!" she exclaimed, pointing ahead toward a German band and dancers entertaining the crowd at the opposite end of the field.

Up on a higher level, the band, dressed in their lederhosen sat in a row festively playing their brass instruments. The women below, dressed in their traditional Dirndl, danced merrily along the makeshift wooden dance floor.

Matteo poked his head into one of the beer stands and returned with two steins. The fluffy white foam spilled over the sides as he handed one to Tora. They lifted and clicked them together, then took a sip.

Matteo curled his upper lip to Tora to let her know she had a foamy mustache. Tora stuck out her tongue and ran it along the top of her lip. Swiping it off in one shot, they continued to walk toward the entertainment.

Stealing a glance, Tora could see the wonderment in Matteo's eyes. It was refreshing.

Matteo seemed to possess a genuine quality of being who he was, not only in his actions and words, but also in his presence. He came across as a what you see is what you get type of guy. There was something different about him, and that something was for her.

"Dance?" he asked.

"Are you drunk already?" she joked. The men Tora knew didn't dance.

He extended his arm out to her. Once she took hold, they made their way onto the dance floor. Neither of them knew what they were doing, but that didn't stop them from dancing to the music, frolicking like children as one corny move led to another. Unabashed, Matteo kicked out his legs and waved his stein overhead.

Tora also enjoyed letting loose. It felt so freeing not to be so self-aware of every move she made. The rest of the night was more of the same.

Tora hadn't danced, laughed or just had a good time for longer than she could remember. Tonight, made up for it all.

"Home safe and sound." Matteo smiled, pulling up in front of Tora's house, Peanut in her lap. "I had fun tonight."

There was that sincerity again. "Me too," she smiled, "and so did Peanut. She is going right to sleep, I bet."

Matteo leaned in. His eyes locked into hers. Tora stared back, not breaking the connection. Their lips met, pressed softly, then they both pulled away.

She thought about asking him in, but it was late. She didn't want the night to end, but it was still too soon. The place they were at was precious. Tora knew once they crossed into the next level of the relationship, there were no do overs. Things felt so good just as they were for now. Why rush it with all the other nonsense that follows, the stuff that makes it complicated.

"I better get this little girl to bed," she laughed, giving Peanut a gentle pat on top of her little head. "Get home safe

Matteo."

Tora stepped out of the car with Peanut in her arms, then poked her head back inside.

"I had an amazing night." she told him.

"Goodnight my girls."

Tora blew Matteo a goodnight kiss and closed the car door. On her way to her front door, she turned back one last time. She waved to Matteo to let him know she was safe, then walked inside.

Locking the door, she found her way toward the dark dining room. Just then, Peanut began to growl.

"Don't be startled, it's only me," an all too familiar voice said from around the wall.

Following the voice, Tora approached with caution. Her fingers fumbled along the wall in a frantic search for the light switch. Finding it, she flipped it on.

Speechless at the sight of her husband Dane, who was propped up in his old seat at the head of the dining room table. His face was thin, dark circles loomed under his red bloodshot eyes. Picking up a hint of alcohol, Tora was wary.

A startled woman met by a man who she thought to be a stranger in the dark, one could say she thought he was an intruder and shoot him. It wasn't a bad idea, but unfortunately, she didn't own a gun.

Note to self: buy a gun.

"It's ok." Tora told Peanut who seemed to recognize Dane once the light was on. Placing her down on the floor, Peanut scurried off to her princess bed across the room, rolled herself up in a tight little ball and went to sleep.

An unexpected tinge of guilt washed over Tora while temporarily forgetting her husband's infidelity. She had been out with another man and she was still a married woman. That all quickly disappeared once she came to her senses, as did her bruised ego and broken heart. Tonight, they were just two people with a history.

The room felt gloomy. Dane came with a bad aura. She could feel it as he sat there, slightly hunched over the dining room table, smelling of some thick, stale scent, as if he had been drinking for days. It made her nervous.

"What are you doing sitting here in the dark?" Tora asked nonchalantly, heading to the kitchen to make tea.

"I live here."

Tora stopped dead in her tracks and flashed him a look. Catching herself, she turned and proceeded to make her tea. The last thing she needed tonight was a problem.

"Well, once upon a time," he said with a snicker. "As I was about to leave, a car pulled up, so I waited. I wanted to make sure everything was all right."

Now he wanted to make sure everything was all right? Tora didn't know whether to say thanks or no thanks.

Grabbing a mug from the dish rack and a tea bag from the cannister, she pressed down the red handle on her water machine and filled her mug with steamy water.

"Aren't you glad I bought you that water machine?" he asked, in a way that sounded as if it were to make up for what he had done.

Tora ignored his question. Instead she went to the fridge for the milk and took her time pouring some inside her mug. She slowly closed the door to give herself a moment to think how she should handle this.

Should she insist he leave? Call the police? What reason would she give, there was no sense of trouble, yet. She kept her distance and sat down at the counter instead of at the table with Dane.

Here sat a man that just months ago she looked to for strength, support and most of all, love. It was sad knowing the life she pictured, the man she thought she married, wasn't real. Her mind created it. A colorful pallet of thoughts that painted a picture which had since faded away.

Breaking the silence, Dane let out a long, loud yawn. "By the way, was that your boyfriend?" he asked, unable to conceal his smirk.

"By the way, is that you, sneaking in and out of here taking stuff every so often?" she shot back.

Amused and oddly flattered, Dane gave a half smile.

"So, why are you here, Dane?"

"I just came back to see if you forgot anything in my big black garbage bag," his voice slurred.

Tora dunked her tea bag in and out of the steaming mug, wondering how she could get him to leave. This had been the first time she had seen Dane since, … she couldn't even remember, nor did she care. This was uncomfortable, bothersome - he was bothersome.

"You don't answer my texts," he said, looking up at her with a silly look on his face. "You don't seem happy to see me."

Was he kidding? He was the last person she wanted to see, ever.

"Not much protection, is she?" he asked, going from one subject to another, turning his attention toward Peanut laying in her fancy pink bed across the room.

"She's Courtney's dog. Well, she's my dog now. What does it matter Dane?" she snapped, beginning to resent his questions, resent him.

"If you're going to be living alone, you should have a bigger dog. More protection."

"I had a bigger dog. A real mutt," she retorted, "but he ran away. If I'd known I would be living alone, maybe I would have lined one up. I'm working on it though."

Dane snorted as if he found her reference toward him funny.

"I'm tired, Dane."

"No tea for me? I miss tea nights." He seemed to enjoy her new, quick wit.

Tora wondered why he wasn't at home; his new home, with his new girlfriend but didn't care enough to ask. It was more curiosity than anything. Was he tired of his new thing as Ali had so delicately quoted Kate that day they went riding in the park?

"I want to finish my tea alone if you don't mind. I have things to do."

"Things to do?" he yawned again, looking down at his wristwatch.

Dane's wristwatch, the same black Movado with the black leather band and blue face, was a gift she she'd given him last Christmas. It surprised her to see he was still wearing it and his girlfriend hadn't picked up a replacement.

Scrunching his face, "It's eleven thirty at night. What could you possibly have to do?" he asked, his speech slurring a little more each time he spoke.

"I'm tired, Dane. I just came from Oktoberfest and did a lot of walking. I'm ready for bed," she explained, trying to use reason with him.

Dane's eyes lit up when he heard the word bed. She could imagine that the two of them alone, his having had a few drinks and his girlfriend at home waiting for him probably aroused him.

The thought of being intimate with him made her skin crawl. She hoped he didn't try anything foolish. For that she would make a scene, a big one.

"I respect that," he said, nodding. Placing his hands on the table, he groaned as he pushed himself up from his seat, sounding like an old man. "I don't want to force or rush anything."

Force or rush anything? Tora would rather have her fingernails ripped from their beds before having anything to do with this man.

"I'll lock the door on my way out," he said politely, then staggered down the hall. "Goodnight!" he called out weakly, then closed the door. She could hear the turning and clicking from his key.

Flying from her chair, Tora ran to the door and slid the bolt across. Time to change the locks.

Chapter

19

Getting ready for her daily walk Tora laced up her sneakers. She was going it alone today, since Jill needed to freshen her highlights. *Maintenance* she called it.

For Jill it was all about the constant upkeep which Tora found time consuming and expensive, or at least for as often as Jill was doing it.

"I'll be back soon." She looked down at Peanut and blew her a kiss. Courtney and Jill were rubbing off on her without knowing it.

Grabbing her earbuds, she hit the streets. Tora missed walking with her new partner in crime, but she was a big girl and if Jill could walk alone for all those months, so could she.

Tora was eager to talk about Matteo and tell Jill about all the fun she had at the Oktoberfest. She also wanted to tell her how she'd found Dane waiting in the dark for her when she came home. It was creepy. She wanted to ask her to help her change the locks; thinking Jill would know how to do that.

Tora could ask Matteo, but she wasn't ready to tell him about Dane popping up. He had nothing to worry about, and she didn't want him to think he did.

Then she thought about running into Jill's ex. Should she stop to ask what that comment meant the other day?

She continued to walk down the long block. It was one more turn before Jill's tree-lined street. Making it to the corner, she couldn't help but peek over. With no black Mazda in sight, Tora passed her friends block by, for now.

The more she walked, the more she thought about it, and the more it bothered her. Was it meant to be an insult what Marc had said? Why couldn't they be friends? Was she not the type of woman Jill would befriend? Was she not fit enough, not blonde enough? Maybe her ass wasn't firm enough. She felt as if he were secretly mocking her, but why? She had done nothing to him, or had she?

These were the things Tora had to learn to let go of. What did it matter what Jill's husband thought, or how he felt about her? He was nothing to her, a nobody. Jill didn't even want to be bothered with him anymore.

Zigzagging down the blocks, killing time, Tora began to have doubts about her plan. She should just ask Jill point blank. Taking a moment to rethink it all, Tora continued to walk and before she knew it, found herself on Jill's block, sitting on her stoop.

The fall breeze blew gently through Tora's hair. The tree branches danced overhead, shaking its leaves vigorously like pom-poms at a football game. A few leaves at a time would gently fall, then whirl about before scraping the ground in search of a place to settle. It was relaxing.

Tora started to question if she were just looking for more problems. Jill had been nothing but a good friend, why make a big deal out of something her husband said? But Tora's mind refused to let it go.

"Hello again," a man's voice greeted. "Waiting for my wife? She is probably out for maintenance." he scoffed.

"No, she isn't home. I mean I was walking and just sat for a moment," she answered nervously. Tora wanted to politely excuse herself and run off down the block. This was what she set out for, so why the change of heart?

"I was over at a neighbor's down the block and saw you here. Is everything all right?"

Her mind raced to find an answer to his question. She had one, she just wasn't prepared with the wording.

"I'm Marc," he introduced himself, extending his hand out to Tora.

He seemed friendly enough. "Tora," she replied, shaking his strong hand. Surprisingly soft, almost silky, *maintenance,* she laughed to herself. Maybe she should think about that for herself.

Marc lifted his head. "Who would have thought you and I would have been the ones to become friends over all this."

Another cryptic comment. Unable to hold it in any longer, Tora boldly asked, "Over all of what?"

Marc looked at Tora as if he was trying to read her mind. "You don't know," he stated, looking uncomfortable as he tugged his starched white sleeve from underneath his gray suit jacket.

Suddenly, Tora began to feel the same way she did that rainy day in the hospital. She pushed her hair back with her clammy hands. Her head began to pain, her stomach slightly churned, and the tiny hairs on the back of her neck lifted. Tora knew once she heard this, there was no unhearing it.

"Are you okay?"

"Yes. I am fine," she lied. "You were saying?"

"My wife - your husband."

Tora buckled up for this swerve in the road.

"You know they were cheating on us, right?"

Force fed a brick; Tora swallowed the lump in her throat to help push it down. Did he mean together?

It all made sense now. The questions, the interest Jill seemed to have in her marriage, in Dane. Bashing him with Tora because she was mad at him too. The thoughts in Tora's head flurried like a freshly shaken snow globe. Her mouth filled with saliva; her stomach grew queasy. She felt like she was about to hurl, but she couldn't be sick, not here, in front of this man, not on Jill's stoop.

"I am so sorry," he apologized, sitting down beside her. "My wife's a bitch. For her to befriend you is sick. I imagine she just wanted information about your husband because he stopped seeing her shortly after it began. That's what I'm thinking."

All Tora could think about was how she could have been so stupid, yet again.

"When I saw the two of you together, …" he hesitated for a moment, as if he should just stop talking, but he continued anyway. "I was confused, so I asked. That's why she took off the way she did."

The pity in his voice made Tora feel like a clueless twit. *The dumb wife.* Her head started to spin. Although he was still talking, muffled sounds swam past her, as if she were underwater.

"Call me if you want or if you ever need to talk," he said, reaching in his pocket, he handed Tora his business card.

Taking the card between her fingers, her glazed eyes panned over what she only saw as dark, blurry lettering. That card could have read Bozo the Clown for all she knew.

"Do yourself a favor," he said as he got up and brushed off the back of his pants with his hands, "stay away from my wife. You can tell her I told you that. If you ever speak to her again that is. I have to get back to work, but like I said, if you need me, call me." Then he walked away.

What kind of person would befriend the woman whose husband she'd had an affair with? Marc was right. It was sick. It was evil.

All the questions, all the personal stories she'd shared. How Dane was in bed, what he liked and didn't like.

'What a good friend,' Tora used to say to herself about Jill. Listening as she poured her heart out, sharing the intimate details of her life. Jill would sit there, looking her straight in the eye, taking it all in. Probably comparing notes.

Tora found herself at her front door with no recollection of how she got there. She walked inside. Standing against the wall, she allowed legs to slowly give way, sliding down to sit on the cold tile floor. All the energy had drained from her body. Her emotions depleted. She was an empty shell.

Peanut came rushing to her side and plopped herself on her lap. She sat there, petting her soft fur, and thought about calling someone, but who? She was never more alone than today.

Dane was defective, he had to be, along with everyone he came with. They were all one big packaged deal. How could he share his life with her, how could her friends look her in the face, knowing what he'd been doing behind her back?

What kind of person does that to someone they care about; someone they claimed to love?

Now, every time she went to the supermarket and some strange woman would make eye contact, she would wonder if Dane had slept with her. Going to the doctor for a checkup, and speaking to the receptionist who was looking at her oddly, would cause her to wonder, 'Did Dane sleep with her too?' The bakery lady, the mail woman, Mrs. Kramer, the ninety-four-year-old woman down the block, did Dane sleep with her, … or her, … or her? … Did Dane sleep with them all!

Peanut's ears perked up, and she galloped to the door. Suddenly, the ring of the doorbell broke the quiet.

"Come in!" Tora yelled out. Pulling herself up, she got to her feet.

Dramatically pushing open the door, Jill rushed in. Her face was red, her cheeks wet and her eyes puffy, but her hair looked fabulous.

"I'm so sorry Tora!" Jill tearfully shrieked.

"You and my husband?" Tora's broken voice asked.

"It wasn't like that Tora. I can explain."

Tora headed to the kitchen to find something to keep her hands occupied and began to make tea; Peanut and Jill followed closely behind.

"Tora, please listen to me. I really was – *am,* your friend," I know the whole thing probably seems so bizarre, but there is an explanation," she assured her. "I would see you and your husband all the time. You guys looked so happy. I wanted to be that. I wanted to be you."

Tora stopped dead in her tracks. Jill, so close behind almost bumped into her. She turned to the other woman with daggers in her eyes. "So, you sleep with my husband?"

Tora was numb. Just like that day in the hospital where she came face to face with Samantha. Today it was Jill she had been hurt by. The pain was different.

"I swear to you, we did not sleep together!" she insisted. "I know my husband told you that, but believe me, it isn't true. I tried to tell you the story in my house the other night, but your sister called. Ask your husband. All we did was spend some time together. I promise! Then when I met you, I fell in love Tor. You are a great person. I am honored to call you my friend." Pleading her case, she stretched her arms out toward Tora, then dropped them back to her sides in despair.

As much as she wanted to buy what Jill was selling, Tora needed time to process it all. She learned the hard way of her inability to read people. Not knowing what to think, the possibility crossed her mind Jill could be telling the truth.

"Tora, after everything, all the talks and the two of us hanging out, husband bashing, you are my friend."

"Was I your friend when you struck up a conversation with me across the street?" she asked. "Was I your friend when you said we both had something in common? Only to find out what we had in common was my husband! All of those walks we took, the times we sat around, drank wine, you could have told me! You should have told me!" she yelled, holding back tears and pushing aside her mug and tea bag. "The one thing we had, or at least I thought we had, that made our friendship so special was honesty." Hanging her head in disappointment.

"I bared my soul to you Jill!" Tora exclaimed, tears rushing down her own red cheeks. She moved to the dining room to escape and sat down at the table.

"I've always admired you Tora."

Tora found that to be ridiculous. What did she have to admire?

"Truthfully, and please don't get mad, but you said you want honesty. I did not even know that was you that day across the street with Peanut. I spotted the dog first and from the back, …" she paused, biting down on her lip, "Your ass looked fat. I had no idea it was you until you turned around."

Tora didn't know whether to laugh or cry.

"And Dane, we just started talking one day. We developed a friendship, I thought. Which he pursued by the way."

More of the honesty Tora wanted.

"My marriage was in the crapper already. Dane told me his was too. He would tell me stories about things you would do or say to him, to belittle him. He said he was, … unhappy."

That son of a bitch! Hearing the lies Dane told Jill made Tora burn inside with pure rage.

"He seemed truthful," she shrugged. "I didn't know. I fell for it. When he stopped texting and driving down my block, I just assumed the two of you had gotten back together," she calmly explained before quickly becoming upset again. "It was a friendship, someone to talk to about all the sadness I was feeling with Marc," she said, slapping the back of her hand into her palm. "That was all. I swear!"

Frantic, Jill continued to talk, rambling on and on. It was all just gibberish to Tora, just like it was earlier with Marc. She heard the voices but couldn't make out what they were saying.

"I think once he realized it wasn't going any further than friendship, he lost interest. My husband saw us talking one day, and that was it. He accused me of having an affair and here we are. But it's not true. I promise you! I wasn't going to get rid of one problem only to take on another."

Tora listened in silence. She tried her best to listen carefully to the words Jill spoke. It was all too much for her at once.

"I'm so sorry Tora. I never set out to do this. I had no idea what was going on. I was dealing with my own problems at the time. Please believe me!"

"You knew he was married." Tora sniffled, trying to regain her composure.

"I did, I did," Jill admitted lowering her head. "He said the marriage was done, you guys were over," she repeated. "I believed him because my marriage was over too. It seemed like we were just consoling each other. Just like you and I have been doing. All I was looking for was a friend. I don't have many friends," she admitted.

Jill sounded sincere. So sincere, Tora began to believe her. She too had been looking for a friend. Someone, anyone, she could relate to. She knew how hard that was, and how alone being alone could really be. Was Dane worth this much aggravation? Was he worth losing another friendship over?

Tora's head began to pound. Needing a break from it all, "I can't do this Jill. Please leave."

Jill stood firm. "But I know you now! You are a wonderful person, a good friend, and your husband was a stupid man for cheating on you Tora. If I'd known that then, I would have told him that myself!"

That was what Tora had been waiting to hear for months.

Maybe Tora was being too hard on Jill, who seemed more like an innocent bystander than an intentional homewrecker. They should sit down, talk it over sensibly.

"What's all the yelling about?" Donna's husky voice penetrated the room. Laying a box of donuts on the table, she sat beside Tora. "What's going on?" and fixed her eyes on Jill.

"Ask your friend." Jill said, motioning to Donna.

Donna looked at Jill sideways.

"She drove up on us talking on the avenue one day after lunch," Jill began.

"You guys had lunch together!" Tora gasped. "What the hell Jill, you never told me that!"

Raising her arm, Jill pointed her finger at Donna, "I thought she'd told you."

Donna's face dropped.

"I mean after all; she is your friend," Jill said sarcastically, glowering at Donna.

"I think you should go," Donna suggested, turning to look at Tora to back her up.

Tora looked at Donna. "You knew about it?" she asked, then stood up.

"Please think about what I said. I'm so sorry," Jill apologized. Turning, she walked to the front door and stormed out, leaving Tora and Donna to hash it out themselves.

A bat to the knees would have hurt less than this. Yet, as upsetting as it was, at the very least, Tora had some clarity.

"Bitch," Donna huffed.

Unable to look at Donna any longer, Tora turned away and sat back down.

"Forget about her Tora. Look," Donna said nervously, motioning toward the box. Lifting the lid, Tora saw one dozen shiny green iced donuts. "You said we need to eat greener."

Tora wasn't good with confrontation, but she was good at shutting down.

"Donna," she began, "while I appreciate you coming here, bringing donuts, I can't do this right now. Please go."

"What?" Donna cocked her head back.

Tora took a deep breath to calm down and repeated herself. "Thank you for stopping by, but I need to think about some things."

"I'm missing Husbands of Hawaii for this," Donna fumed. "I just wanted to surprise you. Keep you company." She closed the box of donuts and lifted them to her chest. "Fine," she snapped. The slamming of the door was the last thing Tora heard.

Chapter

20

After much thought, Tora felt she may have owed it to Donna to have the chance to talk about keeping the whole Dane and Jill thing from her. If it had gotten back to Dane that Donna mentioned seeing them together, Donna would look like a troublemaker. Tora was sensible, so she began to understand the predicament her friend must have been in.

It was possible for Dane to have asked, or rather told Donna not to say anything about seeing him with Jill that day. He must have told her not to say anything about many other things, such as their dating in college, and why he had a snapshot of a boy named Scotty tucked away in his drawer.

Tora knew how her friends could be; she knew how Donna could be. Instead of enabling this childish behavior with more childish behavior, Tora thought it best to do what no one else ever had, and that was to talk to Donna like an adult.

Slowing down as she drove down Donna's block, she could see her friend's large red Ford Explorer parked in the driveway. Tora spotted Ali's white Mini Cooper parked across the street and pulled in behind it.

She nervously walked to the front door, turned the knob and walked right in as usual. "Ding Dong," Tora announced, as she closed the door behind her and walked inside.

Like an old habit she headed right for the kitchen. Ah, the bittersweet memories of Sunday Brunches past came rushing back to her like indigestion. It really felt just like old times.

Donna, holding a large tin tray, seemed to sense someone was there and immediately raised her head. As her eyes met Tora's, Donna's face turned white. The tray slipped from her hands, causing a loud crashing noise as metal met ceramic.

Ali came rushing in, "Oh my god, what was that?" then stopped dead in her tracks. "Hi," she chirped to Tora, screwing her face into a twist, then picked up the tray from the floor and placed it in the sink.

A warmth filled Tora's body; her cheeks reddened. "I came at a bad time, didn't I?"

"Nope, you came at just the right time! Grab a Mimosa," Donna said without batting an eye and pointed to the tray of orange filled flute glasses on the counter. "Let's go to the patio."

If Donna could move on from being asked to leave last night, Tora could move on from not being invited today.

Going with the flow was Tora's signature move, so she grabbed a Mimosa and followed her two friends out onto the patio where she found Kate outside, sitting alone.

"Look who I found," Donna announced, making her way to the wrought iron patio chair.

"Long time no see." Tora smiled, hoping to prompt a friendly dialogue to get the ball rolling.

Kate looked up and managed to return a curt, "Hello."

"Sit," Donna said, moaning as she carefully lowered herself down in the hard chair. "My back," she groaned, slowly sitting back, looking stiff. "I bent down to pick something up last night and I felt something slip, kind of shift. What a weird feeling, to actually feel something move back there."

No weirder than Tora felt at this very moment.

"We're getting old," Ali said.

Kate turned her attention to Tora, who was sitting to her right. "So, I hear you have a new boyfriend," her face puckered.

"I met someone," she admitted sheepishly.

"What type of guy?" Kate asked, fishing for details.

"A vet," Ali announced. "Not a veteran," she then corrected. "A veterinarian. Did I say that right?"

Raising her brow questioningly, Kate wiped the condensation from the bottom of her flute glass along the napkin in front of her. "How'd you meet a vet? You don't have any pets."

Kate's demeanor differed greatly from the last time they were together. The time when she insisted on making it clear, she and Tora were best friends. Today she was cold and distant, like a character from one of Tora's favorite horror movies. Had someone left a pod in Kate's room while she was asleep? Humor had gotten Tora, through many a tough time, and it would get her through this one.

"That's the funny part, I have a new boyfriend," she said using air quotes, "and a new dog, which is how I met the boyfriend." She laughed using air quotes again. It felt peculiar to call Matteo her boyfriend, but that's who he was for the sake of this conversation at least.

Ali knocked her mimosa glass into the plate in front of her, causing her own loud crashing noise. "I'm so clumsy." She shook, awkwardly resetting her glass, then almost knocking it over again, dabbing the orange spill with a handful of napkins.

Kate quickly sucked down the last of her drink and placed her crystal flute glass carefully on the table, lifted her cell phone and typed what seemed to be a text. Setting the phone down beside her, she sat quietly, as if she was waiting.

"Ping." Ali's cell phone in front of her sounded.

Then another ping came from Donna's cell phone this time.

Did Kate just type a group text—right in front of me?

Tora watched in disbelief as both Ali and Donna became engrossed in their cell phones, while Kate sat there, cool as a cucumber, unaffected by what she'd just done.

Wishing she could just blink her eyes and disappear, Tora took a sip from her flute glass and placed it down gently. "It was nice seeing you all." She rose from her seat. "I have to leave," she said, then headed for Donna's front door as quickly as she could.

"I'll walk you out," Donna moaned as she got up from her seat.

The further Tora walked, the more she expected someone, anyone, to summon her back before reaching the door. Kate was sure to trail behind her any second, telling her how ridiculous she was being while trying to convince her to stay, luring her back with talk of an afternoon Mimosa buzz, just like the old days.

The walk to the front door felt like an eternity. The sun shone bright and welcoming as Tora opened the door to make her escape. Taking in a deep breath of fresh air, she exhaled even deeper, releasing into the atmosphere, all the negativity she had just inhaled moments ago.

"Tora!" Donna called out hobbling her way down the stone steps following behind her. "Wait!"

Stopping in the driveway, Tora turned to her friend.

"I'm so sorry," Donna apologized, looking pained not only from her back, but the awkwardness of Tora's unexpected visit.

"Ya know, I came here today because I didn't want you guys to think I didn't want to be friends anymore," she explained. "Dane and I broke up, you and I had that, … that thing with Jill last night. After I gave it some thought, I realized you'd been placed in a terrible position. Then I come here and find you guys are having brunch!"

"I know, I know," Donna agreed shamefully.

Just then, a maroon sedan pulled up in front of Ali's car. Tora could see Donna's body tense up as she must have heard wheels roll along the ground and pull up alongside the curb. Tora then watched as a tall brunette woman got out, closed her car door, and smugly made her way up Donna's walkway and right up to the front door.

Obviously aware of what was taking place behind her, Donna closed her eyes, probably wishing she too could disappear.

Tora could not believe who she saw, what she saw, watching as Sam comfortably turned the doorknob, like she'd done this before. Then she walked right in.

"It's not what you think." Donna said.

"Wow," Tora said in amazement. "That," she pointed to the front door, "I never would have guessed."

"It wasn't only me. It was a group decision," Donna said sharing the blame.

"A GROUP decision? What is this, a freaking cult?"

"We did what was best for the group."

"What was best for the group or what was best for Dane?"

"Tora -"

"I know, I know, the group," she mimicked. "What about women sticking together? How could none of you, my friends, tell me what was going on?" she asked, placing a hand over her heart; her voice shaky. "Didn't anyone think what was happening was wrong? Didn't anyone care?" Tora gave up and waved Donna away as if to shoo a fly, then walked to her car.

"Tora, wait!" Donna cried out.

Tora crossed the street, got into her car, starting it, she rolled down the window yelling out, "Thanks friend."

More infuriated than ever, Tora had an impulse to floor the gas, drive the car onto the lawn and plow right through the living room, onto the patio, putting an end to them all.

Keeping calm, she drove away mortified instead.

Feeling so small as Sam strut past, sending out her message of victory, she'd stripped Tora of both her husband and her friends. Sam showed Tora, she wasn't shy to use the power she had now.

Her cell phone vibrated in her jacket pocket, alerting her she had a message. Tora slid it out and pressed play. Could it be Kate, her best friend, apologizing profusely? She must have felt horrible once Donna told them Tora had seen Sam. Instead, it was Matteo's soothing voice she heard.

"Hey Tora, it's me. Is it okay if we cancel tonight? I have emergency surgery. One of my patients ingested a sock."

Tora wasn't sure whether to be relieved or if this change of plans just added salt to the wound. Unable to keep her feelings contained any longer, she broke down in tears.

"I have to remove the sock. It will take some time." She could hear Matteo say over her loud sobs. "Caesar is being prepped for the procedure. I won't be reachable for a couple hours. I'll call you as soon as I'm done."

After a brief silence, he lovingly said, "I miss you," then ended the call.

What was he getting himself into with Tora? She was an emotional wreck and Matteo seemed like a very sweet guy who was getting pulled into her rollercoaster life.

Her cell phone immediately rang again, and she accidentally pressed the blue tooth on her steering wheel. The call connected, but Tora remained silent.

After a brief pause on both ends, "Hello?" Courtney's concerned voice asked through the car's internal speaker phone.

"Hey," Tora's frail voice replied, trying hard to sound like everything was okay.

"What's wrong, Tora?" Courtney demanded.

Rolling her eyes and shaking her head, Tora had to come clean since she was about to break down once again. "It was horrible Court!" she cried.

"Oh, my god! Is Peanut all right?"

"Yes, Peanut is fine."

"How about Dr. Sexy? I hope the vet is all right. I hope you didn't screw that up. We need him Tor! Peanut needs him!" she exclaimed, sounding more frantic the more she spoke.

Her sister, as annoying and self-absorbed as she was, still managed to produce a wet lipped smile on Tora's tear-stained face. "No, it's not Matteo. It's me Court!" half laughing at her sister's ridiculousness. "I'm the one with the problem."

"Oh my god Tor, what happened! Where are you?"

Wiping her tears so she could safely see the road, she inhaled deeply, then heaved a heavy breath. "I just left Donna's."

"You aren't far from me. Come here. We can talk."

Not one to confide in her sister, Tora really needed someone to talk to. Anything she told her sister would never get to Dane or the women her sister hated—only Ben, and she could live with that.

"I'm on my way." Tora replied.

She disconnected the call and changed direction; headed to her sister's home. Still reeling from how unwanted she felt at her friend's table, the table she sat at every Sunday, laughing, drinking, eating, it was Sam who would enjoy those things today.

Her friendship with these ladies was officially over.

Chapter

21

"**O**h Tora," Courtney cried out, opening her arms wide to her little sister.

It was a motherly hug. The kind of hug that made you feel everything would be alright. Courtney could be that way. Sometimes.

Pulling away, Courtney held Tora at arm's length. With a swipe of her hand, she brushed the hair from her baby sister's eyes, smiling sweetly, "Let's sit."

Together, they walked to the large wooden dining table. Tora looked twice at a small toy resting on the outer hearth of the fireplace that had caught her eye. It was a tiny pink mouse with a red nose and circular ears that belonged to Peanut. Tora sensed the short time Peanut spent in Courtney's life made some type of impact, and this toy was a reminder of that.

Grabbing a box of tissues from the kitchen shelf, Courtney sat across from Tora and slid the box to her. "You have to stop crying," she advised. "Too much crying isn't good for the eyes, so I've read. I also heard stories of women crying too much leaves them without tears, and how it can make your vision cloudy. Just stop doing it. You're stronger than this Tora."

"That was what Granmaw always told us when we would get hurt. She said that she cried out all of her tears after Granpaw died, and all her face could do was make a sourpuss." Tora crinkled her nose. "She said that. Remember that Court?" Tora asked.

"I do." Courtney nodded, "So, tell me what happened. Why are you so upset?"

"Oh my God Courtney," she groaned, shaking her head. "I went to Donnas," she sniffled, pulled a tissue out of the box and dabbed her eyes. "It felt like they had been there for a while. Their glasses were half empty. I saw some crumbs around the table."

"Sunday brunch? I thought that stopped."

"Only for me, I guess. Kate was there."

"Yes, yes, that's the freckled face looking one. Spotty." Courtney giggled.

That was how Courtney would refer to Tora's friends, by their appearance. Ali was the mousy, plain Jane, and Donna, of course, was the manly one.

While Tora sat and rehashed the details of Sunday Brunch between fits of tears and moments of calmness, Courtney just listened to her baby sister without interruption. Once Tora looked to her for a reply, then and only then did Courtney speak.

"Tora, I have no friends. I mean, yes, I have the ladies at the country club. Yes, I have the Power Squadron women from our boating group, and the other women's groups I am in but -"

"Those are friends." Tora interrupted.

"No Tora, they're really not. I can't tell them the things I tell you."

"You tell me things?"

"I can't trust them with certain details of my life, like I do with you."

"You share the details of your life with me?'

"Don't be talking about me down there!" Benji's voice yelled out from upstairs.

The woman looked up towards the stairway, then to each other, and gave a quiet giggle.

"You know I tell you things," Courtney whispered, looking back to make sure Benji wasn't sneaking up behind her. *"Things,"* she exaggerated, trying to hold back her laughter. "You have to be careful what you tell people. It's me and Benji, and I am happy with that. He really is all I need, and of course my little sister," she said, reaching her hands out she placed them over Tora's.

"You have Peanut, you have Matteo, you have me and Benji. Screw the rest of them! They're nothing but stress triggers for you, and you certainly can't trust them. Make life the best it can be with who you have. The smaller the track, the less tiring the run."

Tora looked at her sister a bit stunned, "Court, you just sounded like Granmaw!"

"I did?"

"That was something she would say."

Tora could tell by look on her sister's face she liked hearing that.

"I wish Granmaw were here. I know she would tell me what I should do."

"*I'm here Tora*. And while I can tell you it is going to take some time, everything is going to be alright," Courtney assured her. "Better you found out sooner than later. Another ten years down the line would've been worse. First off, you would have been ten years older," she joked, withdrawing her hands from Tora's. "You can start fresh. The beginning of anything is always fun. You have something to look forward to now."

Courtney was right. If this had happened later in her life, would there be a sexy vet waiting in the wings? Would there be a sexy anything?

"While it breaks *my* heart to see *your* heart breaking, I have a sense of relief because I am positive you will bounce back. As life goes on, and as each day passes, it will hurt a little less. One day you will look at Dane and feel nothing. Well, maybe a little nauseous," she joked, and they both laughed together.

Tora knew exactly what her sister meant. Seeing him the other night, sitting at the table uninvited left her feeling queasy. So queasy, she didn't even want to mention his visit, so she didn't.

"I can't just turn my feelings off. I mean, I wish I could, but I can't. I can't help thinking about things I may have done that drove him away. I don't want to do the same thing with Matteo."

"You won't Tora. He isn't Dane, and while you can look back and say you could have done things differently, no matter how you did them, the outcome would've still been the same. In time, Dane, Sam, and those, … *women*," she hissed, "will not matter Tor. Use them as learning tools."

"And Matteo? What do I do with him?"

"What do you want to do with him?" Courtney teased, cocking her brow.

"I mean, how much do I trust another guy after everything that's happened? I feel like I'm just setting myself up for more disappointment." She pouted.

"We all have to trust people to some extent. I wouldn't want to wonder if everything Benji is telling me is the truth all the time, or if I should look through his wallet and check his cell phone. I would rather be alone if I had to live my life like that."

"I worry I am dragging him into something he doesn't deserve. I'm still processing what happened. Am I being selfish?"

"Truthfully Tora, every time someone involves them self in a relationship, there will be a risk. There are just no guarantees in life; no guarantees, *ever*. Just try to have fun. Worry about all that other stuff later. Enjoy that feeling when you first meet someone, and everything is great. Live in the moment and don't look toward the future. Not yet anyway. Look at me and Benji," she laughed, waving her arms around the huge house of hers. "Do you think I knew I'd marry Benji?"

"Yes."

Courtney shook her head in disagreement, "Back then, if you remember, I thought I was marrying that other guy."

"Bobby Ford?"

Courtney nodded, rolling her eyes, "After we broke up, I thought my world ended."

"You were eighteen."

"I was. Then, when I met Benji, I just went through the motions. I didn't even take it seriously in the beginning. My friends kept calling him "the rebound guy". Then one night, it was Valentine's," she recalled fondly. "He gave me a giant brown stuffed bear holding a little box. I opened it. It was the tiniest diamond," she frowned. "Boy, was I relieved he referred to it as a promise ring."

The sisters laughed in unison.

"Today though, today I would accept that tiny ring in a heartbeat and cherish it. Cherish him."

It was warming to Tora's heart, hearing her stone hearted sister wasn't so stonehearted after all.

Courtney quickly waved her hands around in front of her as if she were clearing smoke, "The point is, neither one of us knew where we were going. He left himself wide open and so vulnerable. I was hooked."

"So, what you're saying is, screw it and move on."

Courtney bobbed her head back and forth. "For lack of a better term, yes. I am saying screw it and move on. I am also saying, don't let one bad relationship, or one bad husband, ruin every other relationship for you."

Tora knew everything her sister had said made sense. The world did not stop and start with Dane.

"Why did you and Bobby Ford break up?"

"He cheated on me."

"What?"

Courtney closed her eyes and pursed her lips as if the memories of that hurtful time came rushing back. "Yep, and with my best friend."

Tora gasped, "Olivia Price!"

Courtney nodded, arching her brows.

"How did I not know that?"

"I never told."

"Why didn't you tell me? I'm your sister."

Courtney shrugged. "You were so young. A few years makes a difference when you're younger. We didn't talk about boys and stuff together. I don't think we talked at all back then."

"How about Granmaw? You could have told her. She was always so good with making people feel better. Why didn't you talk to her about it?"

"I called *Granmaw,*" Courtney, mimicking the twang Tora had when referring to their grandmother. "She seemed preoccupied. You guys were making that horrible iced tea," she laughed sticking her tongue out, making a funny face. "I heard you laughing in the background, the two of you sounded so happy. I didn't want to interrupt that I guess. I don't know. It just didn't seem like the right time. Plus, you guys were so close. I know she wanted you to visit her every summer. I felt like an outsider. I was so jealous."

Hearing that weighed heavy on Tora's heart and it explained a lot; particularly, her sister's mean-spirited behavior toward her growing up and sometimes now, even as an adult.

If Tora's young mind had realized it, she would have included her sister back then. Then again, those times were different. Their sibling relationship, along with their slight age difference separated them in many ways, and as *Granmaw* used to say, 'You can lead a drunk to the bathroom, it doesn't mean he won't pee on the floor'.

As a teenager, for Courtney it was all about her boyfriend Bobby Ford and her best friend, the stunning Olivia Price. Older and wiser, time makes you look at things differently, which brought Tora back to what her sister said earlier. In retrospect, it may not have made a difference in her marriage to Dane if things had been done differently.

"That iced tea," Tora laughed.

Courtney's face soured. "It was disgusting!"

"I liked it," Tora shrugged. "Granmaw always had a way of making each moment together feel so special while we sipped on that tea. She seemed so wise. So worldly for a woman who hadn't been much further than her porch, sitting in that old rocker of hers. Sometimes it seemed like her main purpose in life was to rock the day away, giving advice to the townsfolk that stopped by to chat."

"Free therapy."

"People would walk up the porch, Granmaw would hand them a glass of tea and they would have a session," Tora said, thinking back to those hot summer days with glee, "all while sipping on that pitcher of iced tea she made from scratch with water, tea bags, sugar and lemon that sat in the sun for hours, brewin'. Then, when it was just the right color, she would pour it over a tall glass filled with ice. Remember, Mom would call it Natural Brew. She couldn't stand the taste of it either."

"You mean Witch's Brew! That's what Mom really called it."

"I tried my hand at that tea myself after coming home from her house one summer. I'll never forget the look on my friend Marcy's' face. I couldn't tell if it was from the peculiar taste or from the fear of wondering what she had just swallowed. It was not a city girl's drink, that's for sure. I gave her a lot of credit because it took a lot of courage and manners for her not to spit it out. It was pretty funny. I didn't care for it much myself back home in New York, but on that porch, sittin' and sippin'," she could almost taste its bitterness rolling around on her tongue. "It was the best iced tea I could ever have. 'It was made with love,' she used to say that was her secret ingredient. To this day I really do believe that."

Tora could see by the look on Courtney's face, she regretted not spending more time with their grandmother, and drinking in some of that love herself. Youth had a funny way of setting you up for regret.

As the girls had a moment of silence in honor of their grandmother, each recalled what they remembered most. Other than her loving way and a knack for understanding, both would agree, if they said it out loud, it would be that darn iced tea!

"I didn't know about Bobby," Tora said sadly, breaking the silence. "I'm so sorry Court. That must have been -"

"Embarrassing; humiliating; heartbreaking?" she listed. "They were always sick at the same time. If Bobby and I planned to do something, Olivia came up with some lame excuse for me to stay with her instead. Like an idiot I did. Just thinking about the two of them makes me flinch," she grimaced, "God I was so stupid."

She was surprised to see, how after all this time, it still managed to affect Courtney.

"How did you find out?"

Courtney laughed, sitting back in her chair. "After a football game one night, the game he was injured. We all worried his career was over. The crowd was going nuts, then coach ran out onto the field. The medics came with a stretcher and then the ambulance arrived. He was hurt bad. I never heard anyone cry out in pain like Bobby did that night. Olivia got very emotional, more emotional than me. By the time I arrived at the hospital to see Bobby, Olivia was already there, at his side."

This story reminded Tora so much of her own.

"I could see something was going on. I could feel it too. With all the commotion, and worry about his future, the timing just wasn't right to ask any questions. But, by the end of the night, I knew."

"What did you do?"

Courtney slumped down further in her seat and shook her head back and forth slowly, "Nothing."

Then a big smile appeared, lifting her chin, she looked toward the stairs. "I think it was all for the best. I have my wonderful Benji, who I trust and love wholeheartedly," she said loud and clear, lifting her hands and placing them on her heart. Leaning into Tora, she whispered, "And I looked Bobby Ford up on social media. No loss there," she pretended to gag.

After a few more chuckles at Bobby's expense, Tora stood and gave her sister a tight hug. "Why haven't we ever talked like this?" Tora asked.

Courtney shrugged. "I guess we were both just busy with being busy, but that stops here Tor. We only have each other. I admit, I haven't been the greatest sister, or a very good person in general, but I swear to work on all of that. Can you please let me try?"

Touched by her sister's honesty, Tora released more tears; happy tears this time. "I would like that Court. No," she corrected. "I would love that, and I love you."

"I love you too Tor." Courtney said, her eyes welling up.

"Hey! No crying! Cloudy vision. Remember?" Tora sniffled, roughly pulling two tissues from the box, handing one to her sister.

They got to their feet and gave each other one last hug. Tora left her sister's home determined to work on change. It bothered her she'd been wrong about her sister and Bobby Ford all this time. Once again, proving how wrong she could be about people.

While Tora no longer had her grandmother's wisdom and sage advice, she seemed to have passed the baton to her eldest granddaughter. If Courtney knew how alike her and her grandmother were, she may have felt closer to her; even from a distance.

Granmaw knew, though; Tora was sure of that.

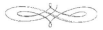

Emotionally drained, Tora threw herself onto her fluffy, white comforter which gave her the same feeling as their grandmother's iced tea. It wasn't just a comforter anymore. For Tora, it was a blanket of love that seemed to conform to her body like a protective cocoon as soon as she slid underneath.

Looking up at her ceiling fan, she became fixated on the spinning blades and constant humming. It hypnotized her, and she began to fade in and out of sleep.

The vibration of her cell phone snapped her out of her tranquil state. She slowly reached for it and read Matteo's name on her caller ID.

"Hello," she softly answered.

"Did I wake you?" his soothing voice asked.

"Uh, no," she rubbed her eyes. "What time is it, anyway?"

"It's five p.m."

"I must've dozed off. How did the surgery go?"

"It went well. The sock was really in there deep. Hopefully, we got it out before it caused any long-term damage. I'm so sorry we couldn't have dinner tonight Tor."

"It's okay. It's been one rough day."

"I hope everything is alright."

Tora appreciated the concern she heard in Matteo's voice. "I don't even want to think about it, much less talk about it. Everything's ok though. Actually," still half asleep, "things couldn't be better," she corrected. "Your day was probably much more grueling, and we're both probably a little shot so, maybe it worked out for the best."

"Are you sure?" His need to make sure Tora knew he cared was clear.

"Yes, I'm sure. Everything is fine."

"I've got to get cleaned up. I've got blood and some sock cotton stuck to me." He half laughed.

Tora couldn't help picturing Matteo resembling a human bloodstained Q Tip. "You didn't get cleaned up yet?"

"Nope. I'm still in my scrubs. I meant it when I said I would call after the surgery, and I forgot to mention on my voicemail I'm leaving for Lehigh tomorrow."

"What? Why?"

"There's a family up there, friends of my uncle, they asked me to pay a visit. I usually go up there a few times a year. I stay at my uncle's cabin and I check on the animals. They trust me."

This wasn't good news to Tora. Weren't there other vets in Lehigh, especially being a farm town with plenty of animals who needed medical attention? Why did it have to be Matteo, why did it have to be now?

"We will have to make up for lost time," she said, hiding her disapproval.

"Yes, we will. I'm going to write my report and then go home and crash. Have a good night Tora."

"Good night Doc."

"I miss you," he said sweetly.

That was music to her ears.

"Good night," she repeated faintly.

Tora waited as Matteo lingered on the line for a few seconds before the line went dead. Tora rested her cell phone back on the nightstand and went back to staring at the spinning ceiling fan. Her lids closed slowly, and she drifted off to the sound of the ceiling fan's motor, wondering if she should have told him she missed him too.

Chapter

22

It had been only two days, but Tora was beside herself for not telling Matteo she missed him that night on the phone. The more she thought about it, the more it bothered her.

He was off on some ranch now, tending to animals like the kindhearted soul he was. What if he met a pretty ranch girl, or cowgirl, or whatever those denim wearing, cowboy booted, big boobed girls were called.

Not only was Matteo good looking and smart, he was nice; a genuinely special type of guy. Women would scheme their way into the heart of a man like him. Why in the hell didn't she tell him she'd missed him that night? She could only hope she hadn't screwed things up.

It was almost five o'clock, the time Matteo usually called. Tora sat, tapping her foot, cell phone in hand, Peanut resting comfortably on her lap.

One minute after five, her cell phone rang, and she answered it on half a ring. "Hi!"

"Hey, how are you?" Matteo's smooth voice asked on the other end.

"I'm okay."

"Just okay?"

She wanted to tell him how much she missed him and couldn't wait until he came home, but something inside held her back, so she hinted at it instead. "I think Peanut has been wondering where you have been. Missing home yet?"

"Well, I may be here longer than expected. One of Mr. Carter's dogs isn't doing well. I took a few samples and asked the local animal hospital to send it to their lab. I went to school with a few of the other vets here, so we kind of work together. We're waiting for the results, and that can take a couple of days."

There were other vets there? Waiting for results? Didn't he need to get back to his own practice where he had his own furry patients to take care of? Tora knew she was being selfish, but she didn't care. She wanted Matteo back as soon as possible.

"I told my fill in that I may need a few more days, and he said he was available."

"So, … you won't be coming home Friday?" If only she'd told him she missed him the other night. Then he would have felt he had someone to come home to.

"No, I think I should stay for the weekend. It wouldn't feel right to just pick up and leave. Especially if they need my help."

As much as she didn't enjoy hearing this change in plans, Tora understood. She didn't expect any less from Matteo, but it didn't make it any less disappointing.

"You're a good guy, Matteo. Do what you feel is right."

"I was hoping you would understand. That's why I was wondering, I mean, it's far but -"

"Yes?" Tora encouraged. *Ask me to meet you there! Ask me to meet you there!*

"Would you want to take a drive and meet me here?"

Yes! she mouthed, raising her arm and pumping her fist.

"We could spend the weekend here at the cabin. I think you would really like it."

"Yes!" she exclaimed, unable to contain her excitement. "I mean … yes," she repeated calmly. "I would love to meet you at the cabin. As a matter of fact, I will work on getting a substitute for Friday so I can leave bright and early in the morning."

"That would be great Tora! And bring Peanut. We're expecting an early snow here, so pack whatever it is you girls pack."

"Peanuts wardrobe, which is nicer than mine by the way, may finally come in handy!" she joked.

"I have to go out back and chop some wood for the fireplace. It gets cold here at night. I will light you a beautiful fire Friday night. In the meantime, call me if you need me. I'll text you the address."

"I'm looking forward to it."

"I can't wait to see you. Have a good night Tora."

Hesitating for a moment, Tora knew what she had to say, but she found it so hard to do without it sounding awkward.

"I miss you." she pushed herself to whisper. There was a brief pause. She understood if Matteo didn't say it back, after all, she hadn't when he'd said it.

"I miss you too Tora."

Chapter

23

The ride from Bucks Falls to Lehigh wasn't so bad. Leaving as early as she did the roads were clear. Still dark since the sun hadn't yet risen, she stopped at a gas station to pee and give her and Peanut's legs a good stretch.

Grabbing a cup of coffee to stay alert, she refastened Peanut into her car seat, hopped back behind the wheel continuing off towards the mountains to be with Matteo.

The further she drove, the more disconnected she felt from everyone she left back home. This trip was good for her. Matteo was all Tora could think about and was happy to drive far away just to keep him company.

"You've arrived. The route guidance is finished," the female voice of Tora's GPS alerted her.

Seeing a driveway forking off to the right of the road, Tora followed it until she reached a mailbox that had the number 79 on it. That was the address, but where was the cabin?

It was dawn now, and Tora could see the sun rise clearing the mist over the mountains. The sky behind the trees was a yellowy orange, and the further she drove, the brighter the sky became.

In the distance, Tora could see what looked to be a house nestled amongst the trees. It was well-lit and rather large, like something she had seen on a vacation brochure once. The surrounding land must have been two acres, at least, and was covered by the bluest grass she had ever seen. It felt like paradise already, and her feet hadn't even touched the ground.

As she pulled up behind Matteo's grey Audi, Tora knew she was in the right place and shut off the engine. As she lifted her head, Tora was pleasantly surprised to see none other than Matteo waiting at the front door.

Raking his fingers through his wavy hair, he smiled. Matteo was barefoot, wearing blue sweatpants and a simple white T-shirt. She liked this look on him.

"You made good time!" he beamed, jogging over to open her driver's side door.

"We did," she agreed, stepping out of her car.

Taking Tora in his arms, Matteo locked her in a tight welcoming embrace.

The smell of his skin, a mixture of cedar and pine, along with a hint of smoke, no doubt from the fireplace, sent a tingle through her body. Then there was a flutter, or was it a flip? She couldn't be sure, but it made her weak in the knees.

Matteo released her and stepped back. His eyes looked at her in a way she couldn't recall ever being looked at before.

"Hi Peanut!" he greeted, breaking his gaze to open the back door and unfastened her from her seat.

Placing her down gingerly, Matteo proceeded to unload Tora's black suitcase along with Peanut's pink duffle bag from the back seat. Once pushing closed the car doors with the back of his arm, he gave a quick nod then eagerly lead them toward the house

"So, where's the cabin?" Tora joked, following behind him up the large wooden stairs.

Close to the front door was a large stack of wood resting beside a stone structure built into the home's exterior wall. "Is that a fireplace, on the outside," she remarked, examining it.

"Yes, and we even have a few on the inside," he replied in jest.

Peanut was now leading the way as she rushed past them both. Making it to the top of the porch, she scurried off inside as if she knew exactly where to go.

Stepping aside, Ladies first." Matteo smiled, bowing his head gentlemanly like.

Tora slowly entered. The house opened into a spacious living room filled with rustic furniture. The wooden shutters of the beautifully crafted high arched windows were pulled back, allowing the natural sunlight to fill the room. Through the crystal-clear glass, a view of the mountainous landscape rendered Tora speechless. If there were nothing else to do this weekend other than look at the view, that would be enough.

Her nose picked up the subtle woodsy scents that filled the home which reminded her of the holidays. *Spending Christmas here must be wonderful*, she thought.

Straight ahead was another large stone fireplace. Beside it was a large iron ring neatly stacked with the wood Matteo must have chopped himself a few days earlier.

"Do you like it?" he asked in a way that sounded like he was hoping for her approval.

With a look of amazement on her face, Tora turned to Matteo. "I love it," she said, her eyes sparkling.

"Let's put the bags upstairs."

He led her to another long wooden staircase and Peanut again ran ahead. It was difficult, her short legs jumping up conquering each step, one at a time.

They entered the first bedroom at the top of the stairs, and Matteo sat the bags on a wooden chest at the foot of a king-sized four-poster bed. "This is your room."

My room? Guess all that shaving was for nothing.

Impressed by his honorable intentions, she was glad he wasn't assuming anything; little did he know that she was.

"And you also have a fireplace," he said, tapping his knuckle on its wooden mantle. "My mother knitted this blanket," He said, as he walked to the footboard and lifted the corner of a heavy, brown wool blanket covering the bed, rubbing it between his fingers.

"It's lovely," Tora smiled, but couldn't help wondering if the wool would itch, keeping her up all night. If it did, she would have to make the best of it. Flattered by the invite, there wasn't anything she'd complain about, not even a heavy wool blanket that would most likely make her scratch her skin raw.

"There's a coverlet and a sheet beneath to keep you and the scratchy wool apart. It gets cold here at night, even with the fireplace on. That wool will come in handy," he said, placing the blanket back down then smoothing it.

He reads minds too.

"Well, I'll let you settle in. I was thinking we could drive into town and get breakfast. Tomorrow I have a nice day planned for us. Today, well, today I couldn't be sure of how long your trip would be and to be honest, I wasn't sure if you would change your mind."

"Change my mind?" Nothing could have stopped her from making this trip. She'd have walked if she'd had to. "Hey," she said, purposely looking into his eyes. "We don't need plans. I'm content sitting on the sofa and staring out of those big windows with you for the entire weekend."

Matteo smiled, "That's good because that may be the only thing "to do" later. With snow coming, I wouldn't feel safe taking you too far from the house."

Tora loved the snow and was hoping for a blizzard. She was content to be snowbound in this cabin with Peanut and Matteo for the rest of her life.

It was getting dark. Tora watched the white feathery flakes fall to the ground through the large picture window in her bedroom. The trees in the distance began to disappear as night covered the view like the thick wool blanket covering her bed.

Flicking off the bedroom light, Tora made her way downstairs to meet Matteo. The room below was aglow from the fire's warm, cozy light. Other than the snapping and crackling of burning logs, all was silent.

"Here's that fire I told you about," Matteo said proudly, watching her as she sauntered toward him. Reaching atop the mantel, he lifted the two glasses of red wine he had waiting, then handed one to Tora.

"Did you have a nice day?" he asked.

"I had a wonderful day." Her eyes twinkled in delight. Here she was in this beautiful cabin with this wonderful man. She was happy beyond words.

The shadow of the flickering flames danced along the walls, setting its light far out into the room. Making their way over to the sofa, they sat, as did Peanut, tucking herself tightly between them.

"I'm so glad you agreed to drive up," he said, turning his body toward her.

"And I'm so glad you asked. I have to admit, I was disappointed to hear you had to leave for a few days."

"Really? I find you a little hard to read."

"Me? Hard to read?"

He smiled that crooked smile she found so endearing. "I find myself asking, does she like me? Does she not like me?"

She fixed her blue eyes to his and turned her body towards him. "Oh, I like you," she whispered, leaning in.

As Matteo moved in closer, Tora waited. Pressing his mouth to hers they kissed. The softness from his sweet, wine laced lips made the world around her disappear. Tora had never filled with such passion from something as simple as a kiss.

Pulling away, he took her wineglass and placed them both on the coffee table before he leaned in again and took Tora in his arms. He kissed her once more, this time a little harder.

Closing her eyes, Tora followed his lead, just as she had that night they'd danced at the Oktoberfest. She could feel the electricity exciting her lips. Peanut, tightly squeezed between them, wiggled her way out and over to the empty end of the couch.

Sliding her arms under his, she ran her hands along his back, feeling his muscles contract as she pulled him closer. He felt so strong. She felt so safe.

Breaking his hold, Matteo stood up. Taking Tora's hand in his, he helped her to her feet. Together they walked upstairs to *her* room.

Tora awoke to a scraping noise that seemed to be coming from outside. A shovel perhaps. As the sun brightly lit the large master bedroom, Tora was alone and feeling rather exposed as her body lay bare in such a big bed.

Pushing away the covers, she reached for her leggings and an oversized sweatshirt lying on the floor beside her. She dressed quickly and tiptoed to the hall. Looking down from over the banister, it appeared she was alone.

Other than the continuous scraping sound, the house was still as she made her way to the main floor where Tora found Peanut asleep on a sunny window ledge.

Slipping on her mules in the entryway, Tora opened the front door and saw Matteo clearing a path to their cars. The snow had stopped and had accumulated just a few inches.

She looked around at the lush snow-capped greenery. The view was picturesque. Inhaling deeply, she felt as if she were filtering her lungs of all impurities as she breathed in the cool, fresh mountain air.

"You're up! Look, snow, just for you!" he announced, holding up his arms joyously.

Tora smiled back, somewhat blinded by the sun and glare. Thinking she spotted some movement in the distance, "Are there bears out here?" she asked concerned.

Matteo jogged back to give her a quick morning peck on her cheek. "We've been waiting for you."

"We?" Tora asked, hoping he didn't mean bears.

Resting the shovel against the wall, he ran inside the house. It took only a few seconds for Matteo to reappear with a green ceramic bowl full of apple slices covered in a bright red skin.

Far back, near the trees, Tora noticed more activity. "Are those deer?" she asked. "I hope," she then mumbled, thinking she saw antlers through the thick cluster of the snow blanketed bushes in the distance. Anything was better than bears.

"Yes, they're coming for snacks."

Tora's eyes widened. "Coming for snacks? Here? To us?" she nervously asked.

"It'll be fine. As a matter of fact, I think you will love it."

She'd never seen so many deer before. Maybe a possum or two from those summers in North Carolina, a few bats, but never a group of live deer. They seemed to be everywhere she looked, and she found it unsettling. The larger deer stood far off in the distance while the younger ones seemed to be boldly curious, making their way closer, little by little.

They could have passed for statues, stopping midway to gaze off into the wilderness. It was as if they were evaluating the area, evaluating Tora, and her intentions as she stood stiffly in place, like a statue herself out in the morning chill.

One of the larger, older deer kept back a little further than the rest, a buck racked with tremendous antlers. He seemed to oversee the herd; making sure they were safe. She'd never heard deer were dangerous, but, in a moment of danger, one swoop of those antlers could do a lot of damage. Possibly poke a hole clean through someone, and she didn't want to find out.

Extending his arm, Matteo held up an apple slice. They waited as a doe emerged, slowly and cautiously making her way toward them. Poking her nose out, she sniffed the apple. Taking the slice in her mouth, she turned and walked off.

Tora could see Matteo motioning to her from the corner of her eye, but she was still too afraid to budge. Not only did she not want to scare them, she was pretty scared herself.

Working up the nerve, she lifted her arm and slowly reached into the bowl plucking out a shiny red skinned slice of her own. Raising her arm, she stretched it out as far as she could and waited.

That got the attention of a tan-colored fawn who walked in closer on long, thin, unsteady legs. Tora remained as still as she could as the fawn timidly poked out its snout, leaned its face in and wrapped its lips around the apple slice brushing Tora's skin with the coldness of its wet lip. She used great restraint to keep from pulling her hand back. A crisp crunch could be heard as the fawn bit down hard to get a good grip. As it walked away, Tora looked down at her fingers to make sure they were still intact, then turned to Matteo teeth clenched.

This was a new experience for her, and she was enjoying it as much as Matteo appeared to enjoy sharing it with her. Not only was she in awe, she couldn't help but feel emotional witnessing the connection Matteo seemed to possess with these beautiful creatures. It made sense, watching him today, why he chose the profession he did. He seemed to have a gift. A deep connection to the outdoors, to the animals and thankfully, to her.

As they both continued to give out the remaining apples, Matteo turned to her. His face said it all, as did hers and it was clear—they were falling in love.

Chapter

24

After enjoying a breakfast Matteo whipped up himself, scrambled eggs, crispy bacon and toast, they got dressed and headed off to the Carter's farm where the ranch hand helped saddle two horses for Tora and Matteo to ride.

"Clyde," the aging ranch hand, introduced himself, tipping his hat and his head toward Tora, "and this here is Molly." He patted the tan-colored horse on her hindquarters. "Over there is Freedom," he added, motioning toward the larger brown horse beside Matteo.

Tora looked wary.

"Don't tell me you've never ridden?" Clyde asked from under his thick bristly salt and pepper mustache as he tightly fastened Molly's saddle.

Tora made a screwball face. "When I was twelve," she giggled.

"Nervous?" Clyde asked.

Hesitating, Tora thought about it. "I don't think so," but she was. Standing beside this large creature she wondered how she would even climb up on top.

"Well, you can't be. Molly'll sense it," Clyde warned.

Tora turned to Matteo. "Maybe I shouldn't be doing this."

"We don't have to ride," Matteo told her. "I don't want you doing anything you are not comfortable with. We can always do this another time."

If she was going to back out, this was her chance. "Let's do it!" Tora suddenly blurted out with a false bravado only she could hear.

Placing her booted foot in the stirrup, Tora hoisted herself up. Barely making it up high enough, Clyde assisted by placing his hands on her denim covered behind and gave her a push. Startled, Tora sprung up, threw her leg over the back of the horse, and roughly fell into the saddle seat.

"Remember, when you want the horse to stop, gently pull back on the reins. The metal piece, the bit, rests on the horse's gums and can hurt when tugged. Steer the horse with your legs and seat," Clyde instructed.

It'd been many years since Tora rode, even then it had only been ponies.

"You'll get it," Matteo assured her, mounting his horse like a pro. "Thanks Clyde," Matteo said, giving the old ranch hand a thumbs up.

With Matteo and Freedom leading the way, Molly instinctively followed. They took the bridle path that began at the back of the farm and cut through to the woods. Sitting up high on this huge creature, Tora thought it best to let Molly take the reins so to speak.

Tora found it enchanting as their horses gracefully started down the tree lined trail, leaving only their hoof prints behind in the untouched snow.

Protectively, Matteo would look back every few minutes to make sure Tora and Molly weren't too far behind.

This place, this experience, was so new to Tora and it made her feel alive. Matteo was kind enough to introduce her to his world, and she welcomed it with open arms.

"Let's stop. The horses need to drink," Matteo called out over his shoulder as he led them to a creek.

"If I get off, I'm not sure I can get back on!" she laughed.

Matteo hopped off his horse and left Freedom for a moment to help Tora. Molly, who stopped where she was, seemed to lean to her side as if she were helping Tora to dismount.

Tora held onto the saddle horn tightly as she swung her leg over and carefully lowered herself down into Matteo's muscular arms, then slid down the front of his body until her feet safely touched the ground.

"Whew! Just getting on and off is a workout."

"You'd get used to it after a while," Matteo said. He took both reins in his hand and walked the horses to a tree near the lake, then tied them to it.

Tora followed, laughing as she kicked out her legs. "I feel like I'm still on her."

The horses sipped the water and rested, while Matteo and Tora took a break themselves to sit on a long thick log near the water. It was easy to become captivated by the lulling sounds of the glistening water trickling over the rocks.

"The horses won't suddenly trot off, will they?" Tora asked.

"I hope not. I tied them up pretty good. Mr. Carter spends time with his horses, and they've been trained well. I've ridden Freedom before, so he knows the drill." He glanced over at his horse, standing proudly by the lake basking in the warm sun. "Molly is his faithful companion. If Freedom stays, Molly stays."

"I hope we don't run into any alligators over here," she winked, reminding Matteo about the story he told that night they'd had their first date.

He let out a hardy laugh and inched his way closer to Tora to put his arm around her.

Tora turned her head and looked at Matteo. "Thank you for inviting me to join you. This is all so amazing."

Inhaling deeply, Matteo let out a relaxed sigh, "I grew up with all of this. I feel so at peace here. It keeps me grounded," he said, looking up at the skies. "You forget how beautiful this world is when you're in the city all the time."

Hearing a slight rustle, Tora saw Matteo taking notice of Freedom who appeared a little antsy. Matteo quickly rose to his feet. "Time to head back," he announced as he stood. He patted his back pocket as if to check for something before he untied the reins and led Freedom and Molly to level ground.

"Everything okay?" Tora asked, brushing off the seat of her pants.

"Yes. Freedom is just letting me know it is time for us to leave."

Taking the reins from Matteo, Tora firmly latched onto the horn of the saddle. Sliding her foot inside the leather cup, Tora hoisted herself up high. Throwing her leg over to the other side, she sank into the saddle successfully.

"A pro already!" Matteo called out, then hopped onto Freedom with the swiftness and ease of a cowboy. They trotted off, a little faster this time, back down the trail toward the Carter's.

Chapter

25

"The lab just text me," Matteo said, walking into the living room to join Tora and Peanut on the sofa. "All is well. I can get back to the city."

"I can't believe how fast this weekend went," she said, sinking back into the sofa.

"Could you see yourself living in this environment?" he asked, sitting beside her.

She answered without hesitation, "Yes, I could."

"When the weather gets warmer, maybe we could come up together; fish by the lake?"

Tora smiled. "I would love that."

"Maybe next time you can ride Freedom."

"Uh … Freedom is gigantic, I may throw my hip out. Maybe Freedom Junior?"

"We'll have to ask Molly about that," Matteo grinned.

A lightning storm was expected in the area and they camped out in the living room to watch it. Together they sat silently, both waiting to catch the flashes of light spearing through the pitch-black night sky.

Tora heard a familiar rumbling coming from the kitchen and turned to Matteo in surprise. As the sound became a low whistle, Tora's face lit up. "You like tea?"

"Yes. It just so happens I do."

"Stay right there!" she said, jumping up. "I'll get it," and darted off into the kitchen.

In the cabinets over the sink, she spotted a box of Farmer's Tea and two brown mugs. She placed one tea bag in each mug, hurried to the stove, turned the knob off and lifted the wooden handle of the old Dutch copper hammered tea kettle. "I love this kettle," Tora called out as she carefully poured steaming water into the mugs.

She missed the conventional way of making tea at home. Not only did it seem to stay hotter longer, she liked the way a kettle looked resting atop a stove. She had been using her water dispenser at home for convenience, and to show her appreciation to Dane when he'd brought it home for her. Tora had since done away with her kettle. Now she was considering purchasing a new one and getting rid of the water dispenser all together.

Resting the kettle back on the stove, she opened the fridge and took out the milk. "Do you like it light?" she called to him while fixing her own.

"Yes, I do," he called back.

She returned with napkins and daintily laid them on the wooden coffee table for coasters, then disappeared back into the kitchen. "Two light teas," Tora announced, rejoining Matteo in the living room.

After sitting the mugs down on the napkins, she sensed something was missing. "What am I forgetting?" her eyes scanning the coffee table.

"Sugar?"

She batted her lashes at him. "You're sweet enough, but okay," she agreed, disappearing back into the kitchen.

"Where would I find sugar?" she mumbled to herself, opening and closing each cabinet. "Found it," she proudly announced, spotting the small white sugar bowl sitting on the shelf. Then, something shiny caught her eye. Behind the sugar bowl was a beautifully wrapped box. The paper was silver and thick, the good kind. A red velvet bow graced the front.

Tora froze. Was this for her, or did Matteo always leave beautifully wrapped gifts for women who made him tea? She took the box, the sugar and grabbed a spoon from the drawer, then practically skipped back into the living room.

"What's that?" he asked.

Freeing her hands of the sugar bowl and the spoon, Tora clutched the box to her chest. "I guess we will have to find out," she replied, dropping down beside him.

Tora hadn't felt this thrilled in a long time. She slipped off the bow and carefully lifted the tape from the folds that sealed the thick silver wrap revealing a plain white box. Neatly folding the wrapping, she placed it beside her. Lifting the lid, she placed that also to the side, then slowly peeled back the white tissue paper.

Inside rested a silver frame. Beneath the glass was a picture. It was one that Matteo had taken of the three of them with his cell phone that night at the Oktoberfest. Tears of joy filled her eyes. Holding it up to get a better look, it transported her to that fun night, their second date. The festive atmosphere, the happiness their smiles conveyed, even Peanut seemed to be smiling with those little black lips of hers. An exquisite red Autumn sunset served as the backdrop for a photo that captured an extra special moment in time.

"Do you like it?" he asked.

Tora turned toward him, her eyes shimmering. "I love it," she whispered, hugging the frame to her chest. Bursting with joy, Tora needed a release but fought off the urge to cry.

How thoughtful and meaningful his gift was, how sweet and precious this man was. She dreaded the thought of leaving tomorrow. If she could, she would stay, the three of them here in this happy place forever.

Chapter

26

Over the next few days Dane relentlessly pestered Tora to meet with him. Finally, Tora gave in, making it clear it would be on her terms. She had an hour for lunch every day and gave Dane only one option: on a bench, in the park across the street from the school.

Having no choice, Dane accepted.

Walking toward him dressed in a white turtleneck, blue jeans and heeled, black boots, Tora thrashed noisily through the piles of leaves in her way with each step she took.

Dane looked enamored. It was obvious she was slimmer, trimmer, and possessing a confidence she hadn't had in a while. There was something else that was different about his wife - she glowed.

"I'd hug you hello," he smiled, rising from the bench, "but I don't think you want that."

Walking right past him, Tora sat at the far end of the bench with her extra-large, to-go coffee in hand.

Dane meekly sat back down, leaving a foot or two between them. He seemed nervous due to his fidgeting, much like a schoolboy with a crush.

"Can I just say, you look great," he complimented, sounding as sincere as he was surprised. "I see you've been taking care of yourself."

Looking good is the best revenge, her mother would always say. Only, Tora wasn't looking for revenge.

And at one time, Dane's opinion would have meant something; not today. The man she built her life around, thought she couldn't live without, felt like a nuisance. A mistake she was wasting her lunch break on, as she sat unresponsive to his comments while sipping her coffee, waiting for him to get to the point.

"Thank you for meeting me."

Looking at him with a tight-lipped smile, Tora made it obvious she had no desire to be there, and why should she?

"It may be too late. You may not care, but I just want you to know, I blew it, and I know that."

Hearing the weakness in her husband's voice, he too was different. Looking a little worse for wear, Dane's once supple skin looked gaunt, and a bit aged. His lips were thin and turned down at the corners. A few wrinkles framed his tired eyes.

"I feel like I owe you an explanation, or something. Just so you don't think it was you. It was never you."

This was what Tora needed to hear months ago. Today, she couldn't care less to hear his 'I'm sorry speech,' that would put her on the pedestal she'd deserved to be on a long time ago.

Staring down at the ground, Dane began to explain. "When I met Samantha, she knew so many people. She had connections and the ability to push my advancement up quicker than I could have ever done myself. Things just started rolling along and before I knew it, it just happened. I didn't plan for it; it just, happened."

Hearing this almost made Tora choke on her coffee. Did he have any idea what he'd done to his wife who'd blamed herself daily for the stains on their marriage. Was he even more of an asshole than she thought?

"I don't need any reasons, or explanations Dane." Nor did she care for the way Samantha's name so easily rolled off his tongue, without a trace of guilt or remorse.

"I'm sure you don't. I just feel like I owe you that. Not only were you a great wife Tor, you are and always will be a wonderful human being. You didn't deserve what I did. You didn't deserve to feel the way I made you feel."

There was a humanity about Dane today, and he seemed earnest in everything he was saying. Unfortunately, it's all fun and games until someone pokes out an eye. Today, on this bench, was a one-eyed Dane.

"The last thing I wanted to do was hurt you. Hurting you didn't even cross my mind."

She could believe that. If these last few months proved anything, it proved all Dane ever really thought about was himself.

"Then that morning, when I was rushed to the hospital," he began, shaking his head.

Did she really want to hear about the events that took place before her entire world fell apart? Then again, it was what lead them here, to this day, sitting on this bench. Stronger now, she felt she could know; she felt she should know, if for no other reason than closure.

"Alright Dane, tell me what happened that day," she sighed, letting down her wall just a bit. No matter what had happened, Tora could tell Dane wanted, no, *needed* to get this off his chest. Tora could let him have this moment, no matter how hard it would be for her to hear.

Dane looked surprised and a little scared. Their friends hadn't said a word to Tora about that morning, and he probably had no idea of their loyalty to him, but how could he, when having no traits of loyalty himself.

"I overslept that day," he began. "When Kate called, she knew you were worried, she told Tom who then called my cell. I panicked. I couldn't handle you finding out," he admitted, hanging his head. "I rushed to leave the hotel. I still had to drive her home."

Hearing him say that, plucked at her nerve endings. Getting Sam home was more important than keeping a promise to his wife, more important than possibly getting caught?

Or was it really because of Kate? Tora's dearest, closest friend, who probably knew of what had been going on the whole time? Sitting across from her at the dining room table that morning, overly confident Dane had been just fine, tied a knot in Tora's stomach.

"Not paying attention, I walked -" his voice raised, his forehead began to glisten with a nervous sweat. "I walked right in front of a car. I don't remember much else after that," he said, shifting around in his seat. "It really was life changing for me. It made me realize that you," his voice trembled as he looked to her, "you Tora, were the most important thing to me. I couldn't wait to be with you. I would have given anything at that moment to be back home. To wake up next to you, have breakfast with you, watch the news together over the strong coffee I'd brew, and you would drink, without complaint," he said with a forlorn smile. "Then, Sam told me you came to the room. She was beside herself. I was beside myself. How could I face you? What would I say?"

After seeing Sam walk arrogantly up Donna's walkway, it was hard to believe she could ever be beside herself about anything, but who was Tora to make that call, and what did it matter? What did Sam matter? She didn't anymore.

"And I know you went through a lot. I should have called you a long time ago. I just didn't have the balls. It was so much easier to avoid it, avoid you."

Tora understood the words Dane spoke, but was tired of listening. Hearing him talk about how *he* felt, she could never find the words to describe how *she* felt.

"After everything, I guess I just want to tell you, I'm sorry."

Tora turned to Dane. This moment felt much like a death as they looked at each other in silence.

"Dane?" she sweetly asked.

His eyes looked hopeful. "Yes?"

"How long were you seeing our neighbor?"

"Neighbor? I wasn't seeing any neighbor?"

"C-Mon. The perky blonde that jogged past the house almost every day. You know her. *Jill.*"

Everything was out on the table. Why not see if Jill was telling the truth? Tora didn't want any loose ends. If she left the bench today with that suspicion in the back of her mind, she knew she'd regret it.

He lifted his head. "I know who she is, but I wasn't seeing her Tora."

"Dane …" she warned.

"No, really, we talked and had lunch. Once," he quickly added. "But other than that, there was nothing. Believe me. We were just friends."

Friends? Could a man and a woman be "just friends" with a cheater like Dane and a woman that looked like Jill? Tora didn't believe that for one minute. However, she believed nothing had happened, but only because she believed Jill.

A wave of relief came over her as she realized Jill probably had been telling the truth after all. Their stories seemed to match; it was just lunch. Pleased with his answer, Tora smiled.

Seeing this, Dane's eyes opened wide with anticipation, and a smile spread across his thinned lips.

"I just want you to know …" Tora began.

Dane sat, his body leaning in toward Tora.

"I'm ready to sell the house."

Dane's mouth fell open. He hunched over, then clasped his hands together, almost as if in prayer. He sat there, stunned.

"We should probably begin divorce proceedings too," she added, putting an end to any ideas Dane may have had for a future together. Not giving much thought to where she'd wind up, Tora just knew in her heart that this was right.

As Dane sat staring off into space, Tora sat back, sipped her coffee and tried to enjoy what was left of her lunch break and the colorful park view on a lovely November afternoon.

Chapter

27

Matteo stayed in town for Thanksgiving and celebrated the holiday with Tora at Courtney and Benji's home.

They feasted on turkey and cornbread stuffing while playing continuous games of Trivia Pursuit, making Matteo, Benji's new best bud.

Tora made her famous Pumpkin Pie Cheesecake, and Matteo picked up his favorite, a simple Apple Crumb. He kept telling Tora how he couldn't wait to heat it up in the microwave and top it off with a scoop of French Vanilla ice cream. Pie à la mode, was the closest thing to being home for him.

Tora knew Matteo missed his parents. With her divorce not yet finalized, Tora felt ashamed meeting them while still having her married name, McAllister. Tora was a little old-fashioned from those summers she'd spent with her grandmother who had left such an impression on her. Tora wanted to wait until she went back to her maiden name, Blanchette, or that was her excuse at least.

Although it didn't look like Tora's divorce would be final by the end of the year, she agreed, after much insistence, to ride up with him to see his parents for Christmas. He assured her no matter what her last name was, if he was happy, his parents would be too.

Right before the December winter break, most of Tora's students had been out sick with the flu, gifting it to Tora, who in turn generously re-gifted it to Matteo. They took turns heating the big pot of homemade chicken soup Courtney had prepared, especially for them. It was one of their grandmother's recipes, and Courtney delivered the family remedy to Matteo's home. The home they shared while recovering together.

As life itself continued to keep her busy, so did the ties that bound her, which would soon end. Tora kept the ball rolling, and with no chance of a win, Dane finally agreed to sign the divorce papers and sell the house.

She was only too happy to set the wheels in motion. Once under contract, they were scheduled to close in two weeks. Able to end this chapter of her story, Tora made what would be her final trip back to the home she'd shared with her soon to be ex-husband to pick up the few remaining items she had left behind.

Before the sale, Matteo offered to sell his own one-bedroom condo and move in with Tora. This was just another example of how sincere Matteo's intentions were. Willing to pay the bills and use his handiness to change and fix whatever needed fixing, Tora declined. How unfair would that be for Matteo to step in where another man left off? With a memory at every turn, there was a lot of unhappiness, and she didn't need any reminders. What she needed, what they needed, was a new beginning.

Walking inside her home for the last time, Tora looked around the large living room. The crème colored walls where pictures of her and Dane once hung were now bare. The house, cleared out of any furnishings, seemed so much bigger.

A new family would soon move in. It healed her heart knowing her home would be filled with a new-found happiness, even if it were by other people.

She made her way into what once was her dining room where they had shared many dinners and served many cocktails. If she listened close enough, she could almost hear distant voices and faint laughter; echoes from parties past.

Inside the empty kitchen, the shiny stainless-steel appliances brought back memories of preparing those very dinners, having drinks with Dane as they danced around in matching aprons. Fun times she would have missed had they been genuine.

She pushed those thoughts from her mind and opened the cabinets to make sure she had left nothing inside. Finding them cleared out, she moved on.

The last two rooms down the hall faced each other. The one on the left Tora always planned to be the nursery but served as a pantry instead. The shelving on the walls was all that remained.

Lastly, she entered her bedroom, where she spent many a night crying herself to sleep. Now, it was just four walls.

As a faint trace of lavender wafted past her, Tora closed her eyes. It was from the room spray and scented candles that helped her sleep for many of those sad and lonely nights.

Opening her eyes, she found herself faced with an old friend; her mirrored closet. Walking toward it with a feeling of courage, she stood in front of it, a bit confrontational staring back at herself. This was not the person she recalled looking back at her.

Once this mirror reflected nothing but bad memories. Feelings of never being slim enough, pretty enough or just plain good enough, this mirror seemed to have its own voice every time she'd stepped in front of it. Today it was silent. Tora would never have to see herself in this judgmental mirror again.

Sliding open its glass door, she pulled out the half full clothing bin from the bottom and grabbed the few remaining items left hanging. That was when she spotted her all-time favorite.

"I've been looking for you," she said playfully, pulling out her favorite piece of once unwearable clothing.

Lifting the colorful, vibrant skirt she'd gotten on sale a few years ago out of the closet she held it up to her cheek. Inhaling its scent, soaking in everything this skirt represented, she then laid it on top of the pile and secured the cover of the bin.

Tora nearly jumped out of her own skin, when out of the corner of her eye, she saw what appeared to be a woman. Quickly turning toward the figure, it took her a moment to recognize who it was standing just a few feet away.

Bundled up in a maroon wool coat and matching knit cap was her old friend Kate.

"Kate," Tora heavily sighed with relief raising her hands to her chest. "You scared the bejesus out of me," she said, shaking her head and letting out a small laugh.

Kate smiled back. "Hi Tora."

"What are you doing here?" she asked, wondering how long Kate had been standing there watching her.

"Dane told me you guys sold the house. I passed by so many times hoping to see you. I never did. Then today, I saw your car in the driveway. I hope you don't mind me walking in. I knocked. Maybe it wasn't hard enough."

Tora minded, but kept it to herself. "No, it's fine. How are you?" she asked. She sounded sincere, but inside, she truly didn't care.

"I'm okay. How about you Tor? How are *you*?" her expression was apologetic.

Tora had an urge to toss the bin to the side and dance around the room ballet style while singing out, "I'm fucking great! Life is amazing! I'm away from all you fuckheads and I'm in love!" but she didn't.

"I have to say, things are nice. No -" she corrected. Why undersell it? "Things are great."

"New brunch friends?" Kate laughed. Then her smile quickly faded. "I'm so sorry about that day Tora. It's been haunting me. I felt like such a bad friend, a real jerk. It was hard to even look at you."

Bad friend? Kate was a wonderful friend, to Dane.

Pulling her cap from her head, she began twisting it up in her hands, "I want to tell you that our friendship, my friendship with you was real. You and I always connected differently than we did with Donna and Ali."

"How are Donna and Ali by the way?" Tora asked. She would never forget that humiliating day.

"Same ole Ali. Dane and Sam broke up though," Kate revealed, locking eyes with Tora.

It was the typical husband has an affair scenario. Husband cheats on his wife, husband loses wife, only to lose girlfriend soon after. Nothing to see here folks.

Shaking her head, "He isn't doing so well Tora." She continued. "He lost his business. He had to go back to work for Peters."

Why was she telling her this? Was it to win back her friendship; to show Tora she could be the friend she should have been a long time ago?

"Not only is he losing his hearing from working with those noisy machines, …"

There was more?

"He learned he can't have children."

It was all too much to hear at once. There was no satisfaction in hearing Dane's life was now the one falling apart.

A little relieved her suspicions about Dane being the father of Donna's son proved to be wrong, the news of his infertility didn't move her. Dane didn't seem to want children anyway. Or maybe he just didn't want them with her.

"And Donna?" she asked, tracking Kate's eye movement, which wandered off to the side. A telltale sign of Kate's that there was even more to tell, but then again, wasn't there always?

"Donna and Dane," Kate said with an uncomfortable laugh. "Who would've thunk it?"

Those two always clicked. It wasn't something you could see. It was much deeper. A quiet, personal connection the two seemed to share that Tora never felt she had with him herself.

It explained why Donna had always made fun of Jill and why she never let Tora feel completely welcome. They were her competition. The wedge that kept her from him.

"Maybe they never should've broken up all those years ago." Tora subtly remarked. One more secret Tora could not help but harbor ill feelings toward Kate for.

"I can't believe all of us won't be coming to this house anymore," Kate said, unresponsive to Tora's remark.

Tora's sentiment was different. She was more than happy to move on.

Sometimes you have to dig through the weeds when you're lookin' for a flower, her grandmother used to say, as she rocked in her chair those hot North Carolina days. *And those weeds can be a bitch,* she would then laugh in her charming southern drawl.

"I'm sorry I didn't call you Tora. I -"

Tora waved her arm dismissively, "It's okay, Kate. Please, let's not dredge it up again." She was at ease, life was good, and she was in love. Why talk about the past when her future was so bright?

"I'm just so sorry about the whole thing," Kate continued. "I'd ask if you were still with Matteo, but Dane told me that's where you're living."

A joyous smile worked its way across her face, then into her eyes. "Yes."

"I'm happy for you Tora."

Tora didn't react. The events of this past year caused her to wonder if anyone was ever truly happy for anyone other than themselves.

"Always gotta leavem' wanting more," Kate quoted, remembering the line Tora and her sister shared, her eyes misting over. "I hope we can get together for dinner one night."

"Dinner sounds good." Tora agreed, while knowing deep down in her heart, they would probably never see each other again after today.

"Okay. Well, I guess I'll let you finish up here," Kate said, looking around, as though clueless to what else they had left to say. She hesitated, allowing Tora a few more parting words before their final goodbye.

"Take care, Kate," Tora stated with a tone of finality in her voice.

"I miss you Tor."

Opening her arms, Kate walked to Tora and gave her a tight hug. Lifting her arms, Tora hugged Kate back just as tight. *Goodbye, my friend.*

Lingering for a moment, Kate broke her hold and took a step back. Tora lifted the bin, ready to be on her way. Giving one last pained smile, Kate turned and walked away.

Tora waited and watched as Kate disappeared out into the hall. The sound of the front door closing came a few seconds after.

Feeling as empty as the home she was standing in, Tora was free. Leaving it all behind her, she too walked down the hall and out of this home's front door for the last time.

Ready to drop the key in the black metal, weather-beaten mailbox, a large manila envelope peeked out reading Mason Esquire. Inside would be divorce papers.

Tossing the bin and the envelope in the trunk, Tora walked to her driver's side door. Hesitating, her eyes were drawn to her Smoke Tree and its deep purple leaves. It saddened her to leave it behind, but she could always plant a new one. Its deceptive nature served as a welcomed reminder she felt she needed.

Chapter

28

"I got that babe," Matteo said, lifting the bin from the trunk. "Okay, so Courtney and Benji are on their way, then we'll call the Uber to take us to the airport," he informed her as they walked into the house.

Placing the bin down, he turned to Tora and gave her a quick peck on the lips.

Cupping Matteo's face in her hands, she rubbed her nose against his, "Thank you." She mouthed.

"Hello!" a woman's extra perky voice rang out from behind.

Swiveling around, Tora opened her arms wide, "Hey Jill! Thanks again for taking Peanut," Tora smiled as they exchanged hugs.

"I hope Marc doesn't get too attached. He may not want to give her back!" Jill kidded.

Not all of Tora's relationships were unfixable. Finding someone who understood, provided support, and helped her through the most difficult time in her life, shouldn't be that easy to let go of.

"We're here." Courtney regally announced. Her large tan, woven, floppy hat and big, dark sunglasses screamed *tourist*! By her side, her devoted husband Ben, dressed equally as touristy, if not more so, in his purple Bermuda shorts and pink collared shirt.

"Who dressed you guys? Peanut?" Tora ribbed them both.

"Uber ordered," Matteo said, pressing the app on his cell phone. "Six minutes, which will be more like three," informing them of the arrival time for their ride to the airport.

Tora lifted Peanut and smothered her with hugs and kisses before carefully handing her over to Jill. "You be good for Auntie Jill," Tora winked to her friend.

"Next trip let's find a dog friendly place so Marc and I can come," Jill said. "It will be like a second honeymoon for us."

"Kid friendly too," Courtney added, rubbing her small belly.

"Wait!" Tora exclaimed. She jogged into the kitchen and everyone followed.

She grabbed a lump of plastic garland lying on the countertop and adorned each person with a lei. Blue for the boys, pink for the girls, including Jill and a tiny one for Peanut. Next, Tora handed out little plastic cups to everyone.

On the sunny windowsill sat a large pitcher filled with a brown liquid and strings with little paper tags that hung over the side. She held back the many strings her free hand and proceeded to fill everyone's cup.

"Cheers," she grinned, raising her plastic cup.

"What's this?" Jill inquired.

"Try it." Tora coaxed.

As the group raised their cups, tapping them all together, making sure not to miss anyone, they all sampled the mystery beverage. Smacking their lips together, they tried to identify the taste. Everyone looked pleased.

"Not bad," Courtney said with a look of surprise. "Is it powdered?" she laughed.

"I used boiled water, but it's still made with Granmaw's secret ingredient." Tora smiled lovingly to her sister.

"Okay," Matteo rushed, collecting everyone's cups and tossing them in the trash just before his cell phone began to vibrate. "Uber is here!" he announced, clicking off the cell phone alert.

The group scurried out into the hall, grabbed their bags, then rushed out to meet the taxi waiting outside.

"Tickets?" Matteo asked.

Tora patted her purple canvas tote. "Check."

"Bathing suit?"

"Check," she patted the other end of the bag as she followed behind everyone out the front door. "Wait, a minute! I'll be right back!" Remembering something she'd forgotten.

Running back into the house, she headed straight for the bin Matteo placed in the entryway. Lifting the lid, Tora carefully pulled out her skirt, quickly rolled it up, and tucked it away in her tote bag. Locking the front door, she was now ready to go.

As the driver hauled the last bag into his cargo area, Tora climbed into the back of the van.

From the stoop, Jill held up Peanut's tiny paw to wave goodbye as the van backed out of the driveway. Tora waved back. Suddenly she became overwhelmed with a flood of different emotions. She didn't know what the future held, but there was one thing she knew for sure.

Tora had found, what she thought she'd never find again– *happiness.*

Made in the
USA
Middletown, DE